Here Is Ware

Stories

Michael Cocchiarale

Fomite
Burlington, Vermont

Cover image: "Fire and Ice" © Remy J. Groh

ISBN-13: 978-1-944388-52-2

Library of Congress Control Number: 2018937017

Fomite
58 Peru Street
Burlington, VT 05401
www.fomitepress.com

For Guy
(1962-2018)

Contents

A Series of You're So Nices

As I PUNCHED bags through the front door, Mom came to life in the foyer, hands clasped, the strained smile of a hostage upon her face. Dad stood in the living room, glaring at an electric fireplace (a birthday gift from Mom, I later learned) that filled the hole beneath the mantle he'd been complaining about since the dawn of time.

"Goddamn thing," he said, throttling the remote. "Turn it past five, sounds just like a helicopter."

"It's nice," my wife Hollie said, easing off a boot behind me.

Dad turned, stunned by our presence. "You are nice," he said. "This . . . this is a total piece of crap." He choked the remote again. "Hear that? Hear it? Goddamn whirlybird."

"Happy New Year!" I cried.

"You." He fingered the air between us. "You missed my big one."

"Aw Dad, you know they're all big to me."

Dad's birthday—against all odds, his seventieth—had been New Year's Day, so I, over the gentle objections of my wife, made good on my resolution to arrive empty handed exactly one full day later. It was my puerile, passive-aggressive way of dealing with the man who for years had made me feel like shit.

"Well," he said, "the party's over and the cake's all gone."

I took off my coat and pushed up sweater sleeves, already withering under the oppressive heat of the house.

"I hope," I said, "you'll see it in your heart to forgive me."

Dad stared at me, one brittle-blue eye up and the other down, as if I'd said something that definitely crossed the line.

—⁂—

TEN MINUTES LATER, I sat in a t-shirt at the kitchen table, sipping a second glass of ice water that Mom had put down as I finished the first. On the doorjamb beside me hung two Christmas cards: one an absolute monster, its florid script like scales; the other an art museum special, pleasing and discreet. Frank and Tony—my two older brothers, neither of whom had set foot in the house for years. For something—for anything—to do besides dwell on family, I flipped through *The Plain Dealer,* which was full of death and fire and the perversely cheery promise of deep, deep freeze. In my head, I tried to figure the days until spring.

A series of sudden pops at the stove scared me half to death. I looked up to see Mom dropping balls of sticky pink stuff into a pan.

"May I ask what you're doing?"

She was pleased to announce that she was preparing one of her traditional Italian dinners: pasta with homemade meatballs, garlic bread from Mazzone's, mixed greens from "that one stall you like at the Market."

"Hollie's allergic to tomatoes," I said.

Mom turned, wooden spoon in hand. "When did this happen?"

"She's always been."

"She can't have some just this once?"

"Her throat will close up. She'll stop breathing."

For a few long seconds, there was only the sizzle of frying meat.

"I find that a little hard to believe," she said.

I expected grief from Dad; Mom, though, had such a long and irritating history of acquiescence that even this gentle grumbling caught me off guard. Thank God Hollie was upstairs in the bathroom.

"No problem," I said, thumbing sweat from my brow. "I'll eat double."

"Then what is she going to eat?" Without waiting for an answer, Mom turned back to the stove to bully her meatballs with her spoon. There was no question they smelled terrific—veal and hot sausage, fresh basil and garlic; however, the frying flesh also brought back the many distressing suppers of my childhood. There was Dad, a regular Old Faithful of fury; Frank, spewing off-color jokes with bright eyes and brows; Tony, staining his shirt or spilling a tumbler of milk; me, quietly brooding about not being given the time of day; and, last but not least, poor Mom, smiling wanly, up and down for salt or sprinkle cheese—whatever anyone else demanded. Invariably, she would still be taking reasonable bites of food while everyone leapt up around her, banging chairs and shuddering plates into the sink. Often—almost every night, it seemed—Dad would scowl at her and wonder, "What the hell's wrong with you?" as if eating at a leisurely pace were the tell-tale symptom of some life-threatening disease.

I was about to explain Hollie for the umpteenth time—her sensitivities, her commitment to a healthy diet, her ardent desire to do right by this put-upon planet—when I heard Dad muttering our way, the floorboards in the dining room whining under his weight. Now that he'd had his fun with the fireplace, he was trolling for his next victim, which, for old time's sake, was bound to be me.

"Don't worry," I whispered to Mom. "We'll pick up something."

So, when Hollie came back downstairs, refreshed and ready to endure a visit that she, in her near-infinite goodness, would never admit had to be endured, we trudged back out into the wind and ice (a relief for all of ten seconds) and spent over an hour at the Giant Eagle, picking up stuff and putting it down, before she settled on sushi and a mix for miso soup.

—⁂—

DAD ARRIVED AT the dinner table in a parka and a floppy, fur-lined cap. "Your mother keeps it cold," he said, which was, of course, the furthest thing from the truth. Mom, in a world of her own, spooned out pasta while my wife blew on her steaming soup. After a perfunctory prayer, we went to work. Then, without so much as a dimming of the lights, the curtains went up on the show.

"That's the transvestite stuff," Dad said, jabbing his fork across the table.

Hollie looked up, a perplexed yet graceful mid-chew smile on her lips.

"She-He."

"Sushi," I said. "You know the name for it."

Dad grunted. "Why's she not eating what we're eating?"

"Hollie's allergic to tomatoes."

Mom cleared her throat. "Is that the kind with fish?"

"The kind with fish?" Dad muttered. "They're all fish! What the hell you think He-She means?"

"This, actually, is a California roll," Hollie said, adding a tablespoon more of sweetener to her smile. "It's vegetarian."

"No tomatoes, no meat?" Dad pushed his cap to the floor. "Who the hell's allergic to meat?"

"Hollie," I said, "believes that meat is not, let's see . . . the most environmentally conscious choice one can make."

Dad swallowed hard, but the meatball—poor thing—did not give up without a fight. "I'm not," he coughed, "I'm not going to sit here and be judged."

"Who's judging? I'm just saying we all have . . . are entitled to our . . . preferences."

"Preferences," he spat, as if the word were a name for a person whose color he didn't like.

We ate in a silence that I knew was not peace or even détente but simply a pause that allowed Dad to muster strength for his next rant.

"So Hollie," Mom said. "Matthew tells me you're going back to school?"

Hollie nodded excitedly. As she spoke about SUNY's "amazing" graduate program, about her ultimate dream of a career working to make our Great Lakes pure, Mom carefully sliced a meatball in four, eased tines into a piece, and raised the fork to her lips. She bobbed her head, smiled, and still the fork hovered, inches from her thin, dry lips. I counted in my head to three, and, right on cue, Dad turned to Mom and growled, "Put it in already!"

Mom froze. After a long, awkward time, she touched fork to teeth.

Hollie was shaken, but she could not keep from adding: "We need to become better stewards of our natural world."

"You know the best thing about nature?" Dad said.

"Maple syrup?" I said.

"NO GODDAMN PEOPLE!"

"He wants to go live on a mountain," I explained, remembering well an oft-repeated dream of his.

"Not a *mountain*. The White Mountains."

"Goes without saying."

Dad hardly spoke of his past, so I was surprised to hear him go on about a few idyllic summers of his youth, which he'd spent on Mt. Moosilauke with a long-dead aunt and uncle. Fishing, bareback horse riding, blackening small game over a spit. What came across was a fact I could neither appreciate nor believe: that my ornery, close-minded father had once been a boy. That—for a time—he'd been someone else altogether.

I looked at Mom. "And what does your loving wife think about such a scheme?" I smiled, winked, thinking we might be able to play this whole thing for laughs.

"I've been married forty-one years. Don't you think I've shared enough of my goddamn life?" Dad unzipped his parka and punched his arms out of marshmallowy sleeves, ending his performance with a flourish.

I glanced at Hollie, her smile more sugary than ever. If I hadn't known better, I would have thought she'd borrowed a few extra teeth from one of her equally sweet siblings.

"The truth is, he's tired of the neighborhood," Mom said. "Too many 'new elements.'"

Frank, my oldest brother—the varsity wrestler, the bench-pressing bully—had fled years ago to San Antonio, and Tony, for years the quiet, clumsy soul who only ever wanted everyone to get along, was (last I heard) in the Pacific Northwest. And me? Because I'd managed only to get as far as dreary, snow-haunted Buffalo—a place at times more sadly Cleveland than Cleveland itself—I wasn't inclined to be sympathetic.

"You been out there?" Dad tore at a piece of garlic bread with his teeth. "You seen those people?"

Hollie said, "I find your block pleasantly—"

"The boom-BOOM-boom that craps out their car windows? The way they stare at you when all you're trying to do is get the paper from the porch?"

"Those people," I said, sensing Hollie grow still to my left. "Just say it: the browns and the blacks."

Dad brought a saucy megaphone of rigatoni to his mouth. "I mean every goddamn body! The blues, the greens, the fruit loopin' rainbows . . ."

I laughed. Keep it light, keep it light, I kept telling myself. "Okay, okay—go live on this mountain in the middle of God knows where. How do you suppose you're going to get to the Clinic?"

"What good are they doing me now?" He rattled the container in which Mom kept his pharmaceutical trail mix. "Hear 'em? Thirty-two goddamn pills a day."

Dad had always been a "pull-yourself-up-by-the-bootstraps" kind of guy. In recent years, though, as ailments piled up like post-holiday trash, he found scapegoats wherever he could: Mom, of course, because of her convenient proximity; the doctors, because of their inscrutable accents; the pills and capsules, because of their shameful side effects; Frank and Tony, because of their filial betrayals; and me because of my attitude and, when he remembered the fact, my suspiciously skinned wife.

"Those meds," I said, "are what's keeping you alive."

"For what?"

"Hmmm. For all your future grandchildren?"

Dad's laugh sounded more like a clearing of the throat. He fingered his sternum—a slow, deep, digging motion between the buttons of his flannel shirt. "That's a good one, Matty. A classic. Makes me wonder why I've always liked you the least."

"Do you recycle?" Hollie asked, holding up her empty bottle of fruit-infused water.

Somehow, we had survived dinner. Mom now sagged at the sink before a stack of plates, and Dad was half way to the back room TV. I had just begun to think we were in the clear.

"Recycle?" he said, turning, losing his balance, throwing up a hand against the jamb to keep from tumbling to the floor. "If that's not the scam of the century . . ."

"Scam?" Hollie was too taken aback to smile.

"It all goes in the same stinking heap."

"Actually, Mr. Rapone, that's a . . . popular misconception."

"Well, it's a mute issue. Cleveland doesn't recycle."

"Moot," I said, unable to help myself.

Dad eyes went up and down at me.

"You could . . . well, do it on your own."

"What's in it for me?"

I touched Hollie's arm, knowing full well it was too late. She'd spied an opening, and, as usual, her dark brown eyes went gooey with hope. She began by listing the benefits for everyone—less waste in landfills, less oil used, a reduction of greenhouse gas.

"Ha, global warming?" Dad jabbed a finger at the kitchen window. "Tell it to the goddamn winter we're having."

My wife smiled. She swallowed. She switched gears, emphasizing the simplicity of the process. "They mix some of the old material with some of the new and Voila!—a brand new container!" Hollie, God love her, made it sound like the meaning of life.

"And all this is supposed to save the world?"

"Mr. Rapone, it is a new year. If everyone made one simple resolution—"

"You want a resolution? How about this?: I, Francis J. Rapone do hereby resolve to be the same old fart I've always been."

"Well," Hollie said, beginning to run out of steam. "I . . . I appreciate your position, but I would like to say that, nowadays, it's more important than ever for all of us to be thinking about sustainability."

Dad could sustain many things—irrational anger at Mom, a grudge against disappointing sons, an after-supper belch—but the environment would never be one of them. I couldn't erase memories of him in crimson gym shorts and bright white knee socks flushing his radiator by the curb, the queer fluorescent lemonade flowing past me on the tree lawn and into the sewer's helpless mouth. I was old enough to put two and two together; fearing his wrath, though, I never said a word.

"In case you haven't noticed," he said, "the world hasn't been worth saving for years." He gave everybody those up and down eyes before leaving the room on uncertain legs to watch his cop shows in the den.

Hollie stood by the sink with her empty bottle until Mom came by to ease it from her hand. Next to the waste basket, jammed between the wall and a shelf of dusty cookbooks, was a black plastic bag, and Mom, with a glance over her shoulder, quickly opened it to slip the empty inside.

—⁂—

Later, at a loss for what to do, I searched the Fun & Games Chest in Frank's old bedroom, which is where, disturbingly enough, we were sleeping. There were plenty of classics—Battleship, Careers, Life—but I chose Scrabble, the only game at which I could beat my brothers, and brought it downstairs to the kitchen table. Dad was in the middle of one of his maddeningly regular after-dinner trips to the bathroom, but that didn't keep the TV from blasting away in the den. Mom was in the living room, lost in the climactic segment of some cutthroat cooking show. I'd wanted so badly to escape—for cool air, for a few stiff drinks, for a quick swan dive off the Hope Memorial Bridge—but Hollie said that it was only proper to stay in with my parents, especially on the first night of such a short visit.

"But we're in here!" I whispered, tapping a napkin against my damp forehead. "And they're out there!"

"Matthew, love, you know what I mean."

Before long, Hollie was way ahead in the game, and I, following her triple word score, was staring at five Es, an O, and a W. EEEEEOW, my tiles read—the sound of the stomped upon.

"I've got nothing," I pouted.

"Why don't you exchange them?" Hollie, with no tile worries of her own, flipped through a back issue of a *People* magazine Mom had set aside for her.

"I'll lose my turn."

"But you'll have all new letters!" She raised her brows and flashed her teeth, doing her best to sell me on possibilities.

I checked the score sheet. "You know you're killing me."

"It's not a competition."

"It is too. I'm keeping track."

"What does it matter?"

I remembered an incident from years ago—the three of us brothers on knees on chairs at the dining room table, hovering over a race game like Sorry, Frank in a wife beater driving his forehead into Tony's nose when he sent one of Frank's playing pegs back to start.

"If you don't keep track," I said, "then what's the point?"

"Aren't we just, you know, spending some quality time . . ."

Footsteps. Dad coming downstairs from the bathroom. He appeared in the kitchen doorway and said, "Now I'm hungry again." Hollie scooted politely to the side, and he stuck his head in the fridge, khaki ass nearly in her lap until he emerged after a long, mortifying time with an A-frame of Romano cheese.

"We brought whole-wheat crackers," Hollie said, offering him her indefatigable smile. "They're out on the dining room table."

"Thanks, honey. That's a good combination."

When Dad left the room, I tossed my useless tiles in the bag and drew out seven barely better ones. "Any other bright ideas?"

"Don't be a sore loser."

"Hey, I thought it wasn't a competition!"

Hollie looked back down at the magazine to hide her curving lips. "I'm just doing what I can to make you happy."

—⁂—

In the morning, I woke in an awful sweat; something besides the house temperature was out of whack. "Are we low?" I asked.

Hollie turned, panic scaring sleep from her eyes. "Low?"

"Sinking. The bed. There's a leak."

I slid off the sagging mattress, heart full of dread. If my parents found out about the leak, the blame game would begin. According to the rule book, Dad had the first and only move, and that would mean bad news for everyone.

"Can we patch it?" Hollie asked.

I put a knee on the Fun & Games chest and pinched back the blinds. It had snowed a few inches overnight, and the white lawn, the sugar sprinkled evergreen, were trying to tell me that the world was oftentimes an achingly wondrous place. I understood that. I got it. Still, there was a whole day to get through, and the more we could fill it up with the better.

"Maybe later," I said. "Right now, I've got to get the hell out of this house."

Remembering fondly her own family's holiday outings to MOMA, Hollie thought it would be a real treat to go to Cleveland's art museum, which was at the tail end of a massive, years-long renovation. Over breakfast, I asked Mom if she wanted to come along, keenly aware that her infrequent expeditions into the world outside were all down well-worn paths—to church, to the drug store, to the supermarket. She had a long, long history of saying "no" to such invitations, fearful of being so much as a temporary factor in the life of others. Today, though, with bright jackpot eyes, she surprised us both by saying, "Yes, yes. I could really use some air."

Before we left, Mom knocked on the office door, where Dad was busy with what she referred to as his "top secret project." "I'm going out with the kids for a while," Mom said, her voice thin and nervous. "There's leftover pasta for lunch." We stood in the hall, shifting our feet, waiting for a response, but all we heard was the click of a keyboard, the high-pitched whine of a difficult-to-identify machine. Dad's silence was no surprise; in fact, it was to all of us a most welcome relief.

—⁂—

Mom hadn't been to the art museum in years, and she was stunned by the transformation—especially the massive, glass-ceiling atrium into which she, trailing behind us, unwittingly plunged. She stopped, turned, gawked up and down.

"This is," Mom said, her navy green nylon coat still zipped to the neck. "This is . . . I don't even know where I am."

"Isn't it lovely?" Hollie said.

"It's now the largest free public place in town," I said, falling back on the comfort of useless information.

Mom shook her head. She looked so small, so utterly lost, that I went back to save her, ushering her like a gentleman across the great, unnerving expanse and into the museum proper, where after a time she settled down and began to admire the portraits and lush land-scapes of centuries past. The peace and reserve of the museum calmed me as well. It gave me great satisfaction to nod at the blazered men and women who were there to keep idiots from taking a Sharpie to the Monets or Picassos. In a more formal way, they reminded me of Hollie's family—polite, culturally savvy, easy and comfortable with who they were.

When I first met the Goodwins at an Independence Day barbecue several years ago, I was simply overwhelmed. For most of the after-noon, I hid behind Hollie, shyly shooting out a hand here and there, flashing the grimace of one undergoing a polyp search. The parents and siblings and cousins were invariably tall, with great posture and strong, white, perfectly contoured teeth they used to dazzle me with kindness. They thought I was nice, but perhaps, as Hollie's mother announced while putting a well-toned arm around me in the rock garden out back, "a tad on the quiet side." They failed to understand I'd been simply astounded by them—by the way they embraced, the way their hearty laughter bounced around the house like birthday balloons, the way that, when discussing matters of serious import, they marshaled hard evidence and employed careful reasoning and, when they did not see eye to eye, respectfully agreed to disagree. In short, I was floored by the way that they were human—or, rather, what humans could be if they put some real effort into it.

Hollie and her siblings took their cue from her parents, sixty and absolutely loving it. Fervent pescatorians, avid cyclists, familiar presences on the charity 10 K run circuit, they put me and my office chair ass to shame. Every year, they hosted with great joy an extravagant Christmas Around the World dinner at their picturesque Tudor on the Hudson. Family members were asked to bring one surprise something—an appetizer from the spotlighted country, a beer or wine, a pastry, even a musical recording. The idea was to be creative. To have, God forbid, good fun. This past year had been "The Cuisine of Greece," and Hollie's father, to everyone's delight, had delivered for the occasion a couple of portable butcher block islands, which, along with the resplendent Santorini installed already in their state-of-the-art kitchen, made a charming archipelago to better underscore the theme.

"Mom, are you really cold?" I said. My tone was a little sharp, but I thought it only normal for a person to unzip her coat when inside for over an hour.

"I'm fine, I'm fine."

"People are looking."

"Because," she whispered, "You're making a scene."

I turned to see Hollie click into an adjacent room, eyes shimmering with wonder. Life—I didn't count her adoption, which she was too young to remember—had always been so easy for her: perfect family, serene neighborhood, private schools, enthusiastic mentors, a semester in the south of France. Until she married me, it had been one charmed moment after the next. No wonder she was full of unconflicted joy.

We wandered into the contemporary rooms, where the most stunning thing to look at was Mom's face, which twisted and pinched in ways I'd never seen before. She turned particularly ugly when coming upon a piece that looked like a robot built by a sleep-deprived four year old.

"This is a Stankiewicz," Hollie said, studying the plate.

I smiled. "Which is, I believe, the past tense of Stinkiewicz."

Mom, oblivious to my joke, put a hand to her coat-covered throat. "It's called 'Untitled.'"

Mom shook her head. "I'd call it 'What a Waste!'"

"Well," Hollie said, "Maybe that's the point. To take these old boilers and pipes and give them another chance."

"Like recycling?" I suggested with a wink.

"Could we please look at some more of the normal stuff?"

By "normal," Mom meant faces, bodies, and places that looked like the faces, bodies, and places a sixty-four year old woman might see on her way to Sunday morning mass. Hollie and I nodded at each other and led her back in time.

"Oh," she whispered as we entered the adjacent room. "Now this . . . this is beautiful."

I turned to see an absolute stunner climbing the wall.

"That's got to be a Sargent," Hollie whispered behind us.

A Sargent it was—a full-length portrait of Lisa Colt Curtis, wife (the plate explained) of the painter's wealthy friend. I was not much of an art aficionado, but I knew enough to say, "This man really loved women."

Mom nodded slowly, absentmindedly, eyes in an emergency room daze. "If this is what he did for a friend, I can only imagine how he painted his own wife."

"You know," Hollie said, "he never married."

I glanced at Mom, who began fumbling with tissue in her purse. In a panic, I turned back to Hollie, tapping my wrist. I was in no hurry to go back to the house, but the last thing I wanted to do was watch Mom, for reasons I feared to acknowledge, turn into a basket case.

—⁂—

We were on Carnegie, driving through the sprawling campus of the Cleveland Clinic, Dad's home away from home, when Mom blurted out: "I was just so embarrassed!"

"What?"

"My sweater. It's the reason I didn't unbutton my coat."

"What's wrong with your sweater?"

"Your father. He says, 'Old women aren't supposed to wear so many g—d— colors.'"

"Good Lord, he's worse than ever. Have you checked him for dementia?"

Hollie dropped fingers on my knee.

"Sometimes," Mom said, "sometimes still . . . he can . . . convince me."

"Well, you put it on. You wore it today."

"Yes, but I lost my nerve."

Now, as I did at some point during every trip back home, I was officially fuming. At Dad, of course, the perennial all-star ass, but also at Mom, who'd made it her life's work for the last half century to swallow his shit with nothing more than a tall, smooth glass of silence. Sensing my mood, Hollie dug nails into my leg. Round, damp eyes pleaded with me not to lose whatever cool I had.

"Just for the record," Mom said. "I hate him."

"What? Who?"

"Who else? Your father."

I looked at her hard, tired face in the rearview mirror. "Oh come on. No you don't—"

"I had to say—"

"No, no, you don't," I said again, the words drifting out of my mouth. The thing was, I should have been happy—I should have been hopping for goddamn joy. But now that this crude truth was out in the world, it was like my brain had hit a patch of black ice. I closed my eyes for a moment and had the nauseating sensation of the car whipping around towards oncoming traffic, the wheel useless in my hands. I glanced at Hollie for support, but her head was down, eyes studying her wedding band.

—⁂—

As Hollie and I headed out for dinner that evening, Mom came at us quickly from the kitchen, black bag in hand, glancing over her shoulder toward Dad's study. "If you get the chance," she whispered, "maybe you could take the recycling?"

"Ok, sure, I—we—can take it."

"That way I don't have to ask Mr. Martinez." Martinez was the next door neighbor. By the time we'd come downstairs this morning, one of his boys was out there shoveling my parents' sidewalk and sweeping off their steps.

"It's no problem!" Hollie beamed at Mom, like she'd just been given a family heirloom.

I tossed the bag Santa-like over my shoulder and let out a spiritless "Ho, ho, ho."

"If now's not a good time . . ." Mom looked back at the study to make sure the door was closed. "It's just that your father is—"

"I said we'll take it," my voice slipping into snappiness. At this moment, I dreaded nothing more than another blast of truth.

I drove from the curb, past dilapidated houses that even another frosting of snow could not improve. The neighborhood, it was impossible to deny, was different now—shabby, desperate, a block with more rentals than family-owned homes—but for all his talk about living in his misanthropic mountain paradise, Dad didn't stand a chance of getting out. He was old. He had a list of maladies that stretched as far as the eye could see. In the current market, the house would probably fetch half of what he'd paid for it. He had no choice but to cling tenaciously to his three-bedroom Colonial as if it were the butt end of the Titanic, rising high into the night before plunging forever into the frigid North Atlantic. Thank God we'd be leaving this doomed boat in the morning.

"Sometimes," Hollie said, rooting in her purse, "you might try to be, I don't know, more patient with your parents."

"Sometimes, you mean, I'm a total shit."

"Matthew, please."

"I'll grant you Mom. But Dad? Admit it: he's an asshole."

"Matthew, your mouth!"

I braked at the stop sign by the wire-windowed corner store, my long-ago escape for Cokes and candy bars. "Kiss it," I said.

"What?"

"Oh, come on."

Hollie looked at me steadily, and I had one of those moments of breath-sucking fear that seemed to tell me that, whatever I said or did, there'd be nothing in the world I could do to keep this lovely woman in my life. But then, her bright smile appeared and leaned towards me. I closed my eyes and did my best to savor the sweet electric brush against my lips.

"Full lips," Dad had said, when she'd come to visit for the first time.

"What does that mean?" I asked. We were on the front porch, and Hollie's Civic had just turned the corner.

"Matty, it's a thing I noticed. Maybe it's a goddamn compliment."

I should have stormed off on the spot. Instead, I hid fists in my pockets. I trapped my tongue behind a hard wall of teeth. Recently graduated, seriously unemployed, still in need of a free place to sleep, what the hell else was I supposed to do?

When Hollie drew back, I said, "There's so much you just don't know."

Her brows pinched. "Know? About what?"

"Pain," was the simple answer, the one that conveyed my feelings without disclosing my failings. I could see the word over and over upon a neon Scrabble board—each iteration a quintuple word score.

—m—

My pocket began to growl. "Frank," the cell's screen announced. My oldest brother in Texas, the Whoop-It-Up State. Hollie was in the restroom, and a half glass of red wine had relaxed me enough to take the risk of answering.

"Whatya doin, girlfriend?" Frank said, using his "ghetto falsetto," which for more than a few years now had been his idea of funny. "Where the hell you be?"

"Parallax," I said.

"Where?"

"Tremont."

"Cleveland? Ha! In God's name, why?"

I uttered a few platitudes about parents, fumbled through an anemic defense of blood.

"There are so many better ways to spend your money."

"Frank, I'm a little busy. Why don't you tell me—"

"Actually, I was hoping you were at home. Got a two hour layover in Awfalo tomorrow and was hoping you'd help me survive it."

"Sorry," I lied.

"No problemito. Hey, when you ever going to visit? We've got all kinds of room and exactly zero kinds of snow."

"Sounds great."

"And, most importantly, no madre y padre!"

Mom's passivity annoyed me. Dad's belligerence made me see red. However, as always in my conversations with Frank, I found myself coming to their defense. "I'm a little concerned about them," I said now, doing my best to mean it.

"Who?"

"Mom and—believe it or not—Dad."

"Look," Frank said. "I'm a straight shooter. I calls em as I sees em. If people—whoever they are, whatever they are to you—they're not going to cooperate, not give you anything to work with . . . if they're not going to try to be good or happy or civil or whatever, then in all seriousness why the hell should you lose even one wink of sleep over them?"

In San Antonio, Frank was living what he never tired of calling "the goddamn dream." Through good luck and fraternity connections and the gift of affably aggressive gab, he had come to manage a popular boutique hotel near the Riverwalk. On a New Year's Eve dare, his wife left a cushy job in the corporate world and, inside a year, remade herself as a wildly successful pastry chef. The couple was childless, but evangelically so. When the subject came up again tonight, Frank told me that his vasectomy was not only "a Powerball ticket to a life of total freedom" but also "a bold act of compassion—a real public service."

"You know," I said, "in other cultures, children take care of their parents."

"Matty, in other cultures, they cut off your dick for pissing."

I shook my head. "Well, anyway, if she knew I was talking to you, Mom would probably send along her love. Maybe Dad would too, in his own screwed up way."

Frank snorted. "Love. Yeah. Speaking of, how's that gorgeous love of your life holding up?"

"Fine, fine."

"You keep bringing her back to town for visits and see how 'fine' she stays."

Again, I felt that breath-pinching fear of losing my wife. "Frank, I think we're going to enjoy our dinner now."

"You do that, bro. But don't say I didn't warn you!"

When Hollie returned, we ordered food—complicated appetizers, clever entrees, second glasses of cabernet. This was going to cost me, but what the hell—the least I could do for the woman of my dreams was reward her for her saintly patience. Hollie, chatty from the alcohol she so rarely consumed, began rhapsodizing about Hugh Jackman, the movie star she'd been reading about between turns of last night's Scrabble debacle. To her, he was just about everything: consummate performer, humanitarian, dedicated family man, a good guy through and through.

"What's he been in?" I asked, trying not to be peeved.

"Oh, lots of things. *Les Miserables* . . . *X-Men* . . . plenty of Broadway stuff."

"Let me guess: you think he's hot as hell."

She sent her eyes to the ceiling. "I like that he's fearless. He's not afraid to challenge himself. To be so many different people. Actors must have such a huge capacity for empathy . . ."

"And you wish your husband was like that."

She touched my hand. "Matthew, I love you just the way you are."

"I think he's the one they say is gay."

"Gay? Maybe. So what? He is married." Hollie tucked hair behind an ear and looked into the dining room, head bobbing slightly, as if listening to vague strains of music from a festive party down the street.

I glugged some wine. "Mom tried to foist that Les Miz one on Dad about a year ago. After the opening scene, he got up and told her, 'I'm going to take a crap', and never came down again."

Hollie glanced around the room.

"Why," I went on, "why in God's name can't he go in the morning like everyone else?"

"Go?"

"To the bathroom. Number two."

"Are you serious?" She leaned toward me, eyes gorgeous with panic. "We're in a restaurant."

"But I want to know. There are things I have a right to know!"

I polished off my wine, which was making me feel crazed. Before I could pursue the subject further, the appetizers arrived, and Hollie's mouth made a charming O at her vegetable tempura. My pork belly was barely on the table before I began digging in, filling my mouth with something more palatable than bile.

—◦—

"I can't go back," I said. "Oh God, not yet."

Hollie nodded just enough for me to know she didn't have the energy to disagree. I drove around, weaving in and out of gentrified zones. Starkweather to Scranton. Abbey to Lorain. Ohio City to Gordon Square. I took 44th to Clark to Fulton, past the police station at the head of my parents' street, over the interstate bridge to Denison, to Ridge, and—at a loss for where else to go—Brookside Park, where I stopped the car in a gravel lot across from a baseball diamond. Rose Field—the name came back to me like a long buried secret. I put my head against the rest, closed my eyes, and tried to conjure a less complicated past.

"Tell me something," Hollie said after a few moments. "Talk to me."

"This was a popular after prom spot," I said.

Hollie, still silly with wine, said, "Ha, ha. Did you get lucky?"

I thought about her possible responses to the truth: disbelief, jealousy, thorough disgust. But it was years ago—long enough, perhaps, to risk coming clean.

"Well?" She nudged me in the shoulder.

"One breast."

"What?"

She seemed not angry or upset but vaguely amused. I saw little risk in going on. "We were lying down on the back seat," I continued, "and, well, it sort of flopped out. The girl wore this poofy strapless thing . . ."

Hollie's eyes glittered. If the shoe had been on the other foot, of course, I would have spat words like "lie" and "betrayal." I would have been hammering the wheel, howling my rage at the rolled up window.

"What did you do?"

I closed my eyes, and there before me again was that pale mold of flesh.

"Go ahead," the girl had said, casual as a host offering a bowl of nuts.

"Well . . .?"

All of a sudden, I was steaming. Borderline livid. "What do you think I am?"

Hollie shifted in her seat. "Matthew, I was just—"

"I know, I know. Gauging the extent to which you've rehabilitated me."

"Matthew!"

For years after my brothers hightailed it to the west, I'd continued to insist to myself that my family was neither good nor bad but simply normal, give or take an argument, an insult, or a sudden lash of the belt. Once, when I was playing Crazy Eights with the Fowler twins, their parents started going at it in the kitchen. Inventive obscenities, crashing pots and pans, a slap or two in the face—the works! Another time, Jamie Pirtle's father stormed in on our electric football game, folded the set up like a peanut butter sandwich, and, with poor Jamie hanging from his arm, hurled the thing out the second storey window. "You knew what was coming," his father said, flinging him to the floor. And my first girlfriend? Our first date was a romantic comedy. Our second? A trip to the Metro psych ward to visit her schizophrenic mother. In a world like this, my family was nothing special. Then I met Hollie and her splendid family and realized there was this whole other way of being. As I got to know them, I became so ashamed I wished I could trash my life and start all over again.

"I was only having a little—"

"No, no, you were making fun. Guess you can't help it because you and—"

"Matthew . . ."

"Your . . . kind are so damn perfect."

Hollie frowned.

"What? Can't take a compliment?"

"Sometimes . . . I'm not sure I feel respected."

"I just said you're perfect! You haven't done one damn thing wrong!"

"That could very well be a problem."

"How?"

"If you think I'm perfect, you're not really seeing me as a human being."

"Kiss me," I said.

Hollie shook her head. "Matthew, we have our problems too."

"Us?" Again—for a dark moment—that heart-stopping fear.

"No, no. I meant my family."

"Okay . . ."

"What do you mean, 'Okay'?"

"Okay, okay. It means yes, I agree with you."

"Okay seems pretty tepid."

"Well, the truth is, you don't have problems." I waved my hands. "You just don't."

"We've had our disagreements."

I told her about a Christmas day "disagreement" between Linda, her benevolently bossy older sister, and Brett, the AP wunderkind. Hollie was in the living room playing dress up with a clutch of cousins when Brett, in the continuation of an earlier debate, said in a quiet voice, "I believe amnesty for all is the only humane policy." Linda nodded while over-creaming her coffee. "A new start," Brett continued, voice almost a whisper. "People shouldn't have to hide." Linda, who earlier announced with wet eyes that she had to let go a lovely but undocumented nanny, looked up at the young man with smiling eyes and said, "You make a fair point."

"And then, and then," I said, "your lovely little brother said in all earnestness, 'I'm sorry—I realize your feelings about the matter must be complicated.'" I shook my head. "'Fair point!' 'Sorry!' 'I realize!' 'Your feelings!' Good God, if this conversation had happened at our dinner table, there would have been fuck yous and fisticuffs!"

"Maybe they were being polite because you—"

"I've known your family for several years. Admit it, you're nice. Everyone is kind to a fault. It's maddening as hell!"

Hollie began to tear.

"I'm so sorry. Did I hurt your feelings?"

She placed fingers beneath her eyes. "Could we be quiet, please?"

Spent, disgusted with myself, I had no problem granting her request. I peeled out from the gravelly lot, thudded through potholes up the old Soap Box Derby hill, and turned out of the park onto Ridge, resigned to the fact that it was time to go back to Mom and Dad's but consoling myself with the thought that they must have turned in for the night.

"The recycling!" Hollie cried.

"What? Oh." I had completely forgotten. The plump black bag was still in the trunk.

"We could just drop it off on our way out in the morning."

"No," I said, adrenalin pumping. "I need to do it now."

⁓

I hefted the first container—a big-mouthed pickle jar—in my hand like a baseball. It was a cold evening, and my cloud of breath seemed more like the snort of a dragon. I studied the calm, clear lake of glass in the hole and then fired away, heart leaping with joy at the angry splash. I took another—it must have held jam—and flung it in. Then another—hurl and crash, hurl and crash. Hollie slowly turned her back to me, watching Fulton Road for cops who might be wondering why people were rocking the recycling bins at half past ten at night. I didn't care—I didn't think about a thing until I found the single serves of Southern Comfort at the bottom of the bag. I knew Dad occasionally forced down a low calorie beer (the only alcohol his doctors would allow), but was he also sneaking this strong, sweet stuff? Or were these empties the work of Mom, a teetotaler for as long as I could remember? Ultimately, in my mood, such on-the-sly behaviors did not matter. The bottles were simply more things to smash—the more the merrier. I fired them in—one, two threefourfive! It was like the grand finale of the fireworks show at Edgewater Park.

By the time I got back behind the wheel, I was tired. Drained. I dropped my head against Hollie's shoulder.

"Would you like me to drive?" she asked, kissing me on the forehead.

"No, no, I can handle it."

"We probably shouldn't have stayed out so long."

"It was a matter of survival."

"Your father is old," Hollie said. "He might not have long."

"He's had long enough."

"Matthew, when the time comes, you will miss him."

Hollie, it was clear, was thinking less of my angry Dad than of her own father—that warm, hearty soul. Those pleasantly boisterous holiday dinners, the fun family trips into the big city, the farm-to-table brunches, the jubilant finish line of all those 10 K races. I wanted to set her straight, but fatigue made me diplomatic. "Maybe, maybe," I said. "There is always a chance."

Hollie squeezed my leg. Her dark eyes shined. How easy it was to fool her. All it took was a handful of noncommittal words.

—⁂—

We returned late—after more drinks, after our sudden second wind collapsed—and swayed and giggled upstairs. While Hollie took out her earrings, I fell upon the inflatable mattress.

"Oh wow," I said. "We're pretty much out."

"Out?"

"The mattress. We need serious air."

"Now?"

It was, as I'd said this morning, an impossible operation. Even if we could locate the pump, there would be noise; and with noise, there would be my parents, Dad's grumbly "goddamn" followed by Mom and a series of futile, placating whispers. Within a minute, the gates of hell would fly open, and we'd have to grab what we could and make a break for it.

"Never mind," I said. "We'll survive." I closed my eyes. After a moment, I kicked down my jeans and flapped my boxers for air. "If this heat doesn't kill us, nothing will."

Hollie stood smiling at the door. "Aren't you going to . . . freshen up?"

"I'm sooo tired."

"You're . . ."

"Gross. Go ahead, you can say it."

A few minutes later, back from the bathroom, Hollie slid onto what was left of our bed, smelling of vanilla lotion and peppermint mouthwash, a combination that, despite my exhaustion, I found more than a little arousing. I counted to ten and turned, but she was already out. Beyond her on the wall was a low shelf filled with our family's ancient texts—board books, I Can Reads, Frank's *Mad* magazines, a complete series of fantasy novels Tony couldn't get enough of more than half a life ago. Why did Mom keep all these useless artifacts of our mostly painful past? Why not pack them off to the public library, to Goodwill? Why not give this stuff the new and better life it deserved?

Hollie shifted. She hugged her pillow and released a lovely sigh.

"Hollie . . . Hollie berry," I whispered, making light swirling motions with a finger on her neck.

"Hmmm?"

"Want to make a kid? A grandkid!"

"Sure," she said after a long pause. "Not . . . now."

"When?"

"Tuesday."

"This Tuesday?"

"Brushing teeth, you know, is the first step to healthy oral hygiene."

"Sounds good," I said. "I have to go anyway."

As I unzipped in the bathroom, I saw above the towel rack a startling new addition—a framed postcard of a woman with a long face, a skinny neck, and dense, hedgehog hair. Her green eyes were despondent, worn out, her blood red lips unnervingly askew. I slid the card from its frame and turned it over: "Portrait of a Woman," it read. "Amedeo Modigliani." Why hadn't Mom bought the postcard of the Sargent painting that had nearly moved her to tears?

Why this particular figure—so sad, so anonymous? It seemed such an obvious, self-pitying thing to do that all at once I was furious with her again.

But I didn't know real rage until I looked down and there, clinging to the side of the toilet bowl, were four brown fingerprints, courtesy of good old Dad. I swayed, blinked, and the piss missed its mark. I aimed again. Concentrate, concentrate. My stream was strong—full of drunken fury—but God, those flecks of shit were adamant. They clung like dark secrets, out in the open for good.

—⁓—

In the morning, my head was a house full of banging doors; it was my back, however, that I thought might need medical attention. I tried to stand, but had to call to Hollie to bend me straight.

"I wonder if you aren't overdoing it a bit?" she asked.

"I would like to overdo you."

She smiled, resting a hand against my boxers for one terrific second before bringing her suitcase downstairs.

I stretched. Hands on hips, I moved from side to side and round and round. When I tried to touch my toes, I saw on the bottom shelf of the bookcase a photograph like a tongue between two fantasy novels. It was a picture of Tony in high school, snappy haircut and tie, arms tight around two role-playing nerds. Once, Frank sent a postcard from San Francisco that began, "Thought you'd like this, Sis." When I asked Tony what that meant, he laughed good-naturedly and said, "You know Frank. He sees a crack in the door, he goes right for the kill." I nodded, although I had no idea what he was talking about.

Despite the constant tension in the house, Tony, unlike Frank, seemed happy enough to stay put. He loved school and had close friends he wouldn't trade for anything in the world. After dinner, he'd hum pop tunes while washing pots and pans. Later—unless buried by homework—he'd sit with Mom to watch Jeopardy, either impressing her with his knowledge or making her laugh with absurd answers like "What is 'Come Again?'" and "What is 'I'll Never Tell?'" Once, when Dad cursed a blood pressure pill he'd dropped on the kitchen floor, Tony got down on all fours and said, "What's life without a challenge?"

But one May morning, I drummed downstairs to see Tony, less than a month from high school graduation, standing on our front sidewalk, adjusting a duffle bag on his shoulder. Dad, naked belly pulsing above his briefs, screamed from the porch, "You're dead to me!" Tony pursed his lips. He looked ready to cry. Instead, he cleared his throat and said, "I feel sorry for you. I really, really do." I was twelve and frightened and did not want to understand what had just transpired. Tony called a few days later, while Dad was safe at work. Mom came into my room, phone pressed against her chest, asking if I'd like to talk. I recoiled on the bed, shook my head so hard I thought it would fly against the wall. When the letters came that summer—one in June and the other in August—I looked at the handwriting and tore them both to shreds.

My back pain was still there (in fact, it had grown suddenly worse), but I knelt down, removed the plug from the inflatable bed and folded the thing back and forth, pressing down upon it each time to release whatever air was left. When I was finished, I kicked the tiny blue square into the corner of the room, where it sat like a forlorn piece of cake that would eventually end up in the can.

After a cold shower, I stood at the top of the stairs, listening to

Mom go on about a vegetarian stir fry she had planned to make, an explanation punctuated by Hollie's mellifluous series of "You're so nices."

"Well, you should take the soy sauce. And the baby corn. Oh, the straw mushrooms too! We're never going to use them."

Hollie said, "No, no, please," until, as I appeared at the landing, she said "Thank you," and received the items with her usual sweetness and grace.

When she went outside to put the unexpected gifts in the car, I clumped downstairs, my goodbye all set. I found Mom at the kitchen table, a smear of preserves on a knife, the toast going hard on the plate.

"I wish you didn't have to go," she said.

"Oh, don't worry," I said, taking a sip of bitter coffee. "We'll be back."

"When?"

I studied the steaming mug on her mat. How much of that dark liquid was Maxwell House and how much Southern Comfort?

"I can live with an estimate."

I shrugged. "It's such a long drive."

When Mom's eyes dropped toward the newspaper, I took the opportunity to escape to the living room. Hollie stood on the porch steps, chatting amiably with Mr. Rodriguez as he brushed fresh snow from his hatchback. I watched her for a few moments, wondering again how she and her kind could get along so easily with the world. It was a real talent.

I headed back toward the kitchen to put my mug in the sink, but felt compelled to stop first at Dad's office door. "Well . . . see you soon," I said, speaking into the "KEEP OUT" sign as if it were an intercom.

"So long," he growled.

"You too."

"Watch out for the other guy."

"Will do."

"Take care of that wonderful wife."

I took a deep breath. I tried the knob, but it didn't budge. "Dad, will you open up already?"

Silence.

I knocked once. Twice. I kept my knuckles going until wheels cried along the hard wood floor. The door opened, and there was Dad in his swivel chair, clamped teeth and up and down eyes. "What?" he said. "What do you need?"

To my surprise, he'd not been blogging vehemently about blacks or printing 3 D guns or downloading recipes for homemade bombs. He'd been sitting at his desk scanning old photographs. On the screen behind him was a discolored picture from a long ago Christmas—three plaid pajamaed boys squawking in a nest of wrapping paper, Mom in a bathrobe, eyes small and skittish behind hula hoop frames.

He caressed a photograph in his hands with a cloth. "This removes all the static," he said before placing it gently on the scanner bed. "Easy as pie."

Behind him on the screen, my family's early years continued to play out, one moment melting into the next: my sixth or seventh birthday, a Formula One cake between nail-bitten hands; a family portrait from a camping trip in the Hocking Hills; Dad, shirtless and smiling against a sunburnt Mustang, an arm around the neck of teenaged Frank and the other reaching out for (or pushing away?) Tony, who stood awkwardly with hand on hip a few feet away. I noticed music too, a soundtrack—tumbling piano, like chords cascading down stairs. Catchy tune, for sure. But cloying too.

"Wait," I said. "This is . . . Coldplay?"

"Cold day? Well, it's wint—"

"How do you know Coldplay? The musical group." A few years ago, Frank, drunk as a skunk, called in the middle of the night to say he'd been roped into going to a concert and thought, to be honest, the band wasn't half bad. "They're not fag rock, right?" he asked, voice playful and anxious. "'Cause if they are, then there's something in the goddamn blood." I told him to get some sleep. "You keep on the lookout," he said. "Be vigilant is all I'm saying."

Ignoring me, Dad wiped another picture and closed the scanner lid over it. In a queer, sentimental stupor, I watched the screen for another minute before I had the courage to acknowledge this display for what it was: a dirty rotten trick, a shameless repackaging of everything that had been fucked up for years.

"Listen," I said. "I know exactly what you're doing."

"You? You've always been the dumbest of them all."

"I know. I really do."

"No you don't."

"I do!"

A stack of pictures slid from the desk. Dad squeezed the arms of his swivel chair and said, "Goddamnit, you don't!"

"Fine, fine, fiiiiiiiine!"

Dad picked up a handful of photos and flung them like knives at my head. "Go! Go away you little chicken shit!"

I wanted to hurt him—hurt him bad—but the only thing I could think to do short of punching him in the face was to announce that Mom hated his guts. The thing was, how could he be so dense not to know that obvious truth? And if for some strange reason he didn't, what were the chances he'd care? Disgusted, defeated, I jerked closed the door and brushed by Mom, who was shuffling with beleaguered eyes toward the ruckus.

"What? What?" she said. "What's happened now?"

I kept going—into the living room, where the fake fireplace roared; into the foyer, where Hollie stood, hands on hips, a portrait of confusion; then out the goddamn door.

—⁓—

We were silent all the way to Ashtabula, a good sixty miles from the city. I went from being certain I'd never speak again to thinking I might, if pressed, grunt "yes" or "no" in response to an especially deserving question, to realizing that what was needed was not simply a word or two but some real communication. Sports? Weather? Lunch?—pleasantries weren't going to do the job. I needed to reach my wife, not the cashier at the Giant Eagle. I needed to make it clear that we were together—on the same side.

"So . . ." I said, casual as could be, "what were you and Rodriguez talking about?"

Hollie looked my way, lips flat, face a closed closet door.

"You know, Dad's sure he's one of the illegals."

"Believe it or not, adoption," she said. "His wife's daughter. He's legally adopted her. Finalized the paperwork yesterday afternoon."

"Oh. Where's the real father?"

Hollie's mouth moved as if there were hostages inside, desperate to escape. In the silence that followed, my thoughtless question grew— an ugly, oppressive balloon between us.

"He is the real father," she said at last, laying out each word in a careful, controlled tone.

"Lord . . . now you're angry."

"No, Matthew. I'm hurt. I'm in pain."

"Fair enough."

As we passed into Pennsylvania, it began to snow—slow, delicate flakes that failed to make an impression. I turned down the heat, angled the vent away from my burning face.

"I remember when they came to the orphanage," Hollie said.

It took me a few seconds to realize she was talking not about Rodriguez but about her own parents—her own adoption day. Eagerly, I nodded. I told myself not to say another word.

"You know I was three and a half. Old enough to be aware of things. I'd been told for weeks by the caretakers that I'd be going away with a new family to the greatest country in the world. It didn't mean much to me at the time. I had friends—there was one girl, I can't remember her name but she had a cleft palate, and we played together with hand gestures and smiles. She never said a word. Then one day after breakfast, I was called in from the playground to see this tall white man and woman standing in front of me, wiping away tears. The woman bent to give me a teddy bear, but I was more interested in these strange new faces. Why were they crying? What had happened to them? I took their hands. I squeezed the man's neck when he picked me up. I thought they could use my help."

I nodded. I was trying very hard to be good.

"Everything was okay until the airport, when I saw this woman on the other side of the waiting room. I caught her eye, and she smiled. That face—the eyes, hair, and skin—they were just like mine, and I remember . . . I remember thinking, on some level, I know I was thinking . . . 'mother.'"

Hollie stopped to place fingers under her eyes. "I was off. I was moving toward her and she—I'm almost sure of it—held out her arms. Then, out of nowhere, a big hand appeared in front of me, and like that I was up in the air and facing back from where I'd come. When I turned, that woman was looking down at a magazine drooped over her lap. Like I was no longer even there. I cried, Mom said. Boy did I cry. In fact, it wasn't until we were well over the ocean that I stopped."

She gently palmed her eyes.

"Oh, and later, there were moments. Difficult times. I can't tell you how often I dreamed of that woman—her smile, her soft hands, the flap of the magazine. Sometimes, I woke screaming. Once, when I was a thirteen or fourteen, I'm ashamed to say I threw a piece of Mom's best china on the kitchen floor. I said I hated them both for stealing me away."

I nodded and nodded. Suddenly, it seemed like hours since I'd heard more than enough.

She patted my leg. "I'm sorry. I just wanted you to know. I thought you should know where I'm coming from."

Directly ahead, traffic had begun to slow down in the face of harder snow. I sped up, blinkered into the left lane to pass a line of doddering vehicles. Seventy. Seventy-five. However fast I drove, I knew I couldn't outrun an old story that caught up with me from time to time. I was twelve. In seventh grade. The boiler at school had burst, and I'd come home early. Mom was in the basement—her sanctuary—washing clothes and said she'd be up in a bit. I went upstairs to change and heard giggles from Tony's room, the rough loosening of clothes, the dink of metal on the hardwood floor. Twenty minutes passed, and he and his best friend came downstairs, plopping unapologetically on either side of me to watch the second half of Scooby Doo. After a time, I gathered the courage to glance at the friend and saw that the zipper of his pants was down, the fly a dark, gold-toothed mouth ready to eat me alive. At a commercial break, I ran up to the bathroom and gagged into the toilet. The next day with Dad in the car, going to pick up a bucket of fried chicken, I, in so many words, told him what I'd heard and what I thought it meant. For the last few months, he'd been on my case about absolutely everything—poor grades in math, striking out in a softball game, the inability to find the latch on the hood of the car—and blurting out a name, a word, and an act seemed like a clear cut way to claw back into his good graces.

"Your turn," Hollie said, the sun back in her eyes. "Tell me something new."

"I love you," I said.

"That's not new."

"I love you more than ever?"

As Hollie touched my leg again, I thought about Tony, about how he was far better off wherever the hell he was. By now, he had to have found a boyfriend, a lover, a partner. Maybe even a child, a dapper little boy—they were known to do that as well.

"Matthew, you're so nice."

Yes, that was the truth: Tony had it made. I was no hero, of course, but hadn't I in large part helped to break him loose? Because of me, he was—and had been for years—dancing in the open, the same person inside and out. He'd never need to change a thing for anyone ever again.

"You know that, don't you?"

"I'm not going to argue," I said, flicking wipers at the snow. The flakes returned with a vengeance, and, in the silence that settled between us, I wondered how long I could go before I'd need to clean the shield again.

Mei Wenti

ON THEIR THIRD trip to the steam tables, Yanmei wheelied up to a baby octopus on ice, would have touched it, in fact, had not Paul, darting from behind, lightly caught her wrist.

"Can I have that?" she asked.

"Trust me: you don't want to."

As his daughter moved down the line, Paul stared at the livid purple skin, the white, donut-shaped suction cups. He imagined the creature leaping from the table and attaching to his face, drawing out the breath he was already finding difficult to catch.

After much deliberation, Yanmei settled on one flaccid dumpling and a ladle full of duck sauce, which was of course way too much, but Paul found himself becoming more permissive as their afternoon drew to a close.

Back at the table, he dipped a shard of almond cookie in lukewarm tea while Yanmei swam her dumpling through orange goo.

"You really didn't want that," he said, longing to be stern—looking upon this moment as a perfect opportunity to cultivate just such a tone.

Yanmei lifted the dumpling with her chopsticks to prove other-wise, but the thing flopped like a fish back on the plate. With a giggle, she went right back to prodding and chasing it around.

"You're full, aren't you?"

"I am this full," she said, chopping a hand against the gold buttons of her designer overalls, the same ones that Yanmei had worn a month ago, when he had been painting the living room ceiling and she, having just returned with Jess from the King of Prussia Mall, burst through the door holding up a pink shirt embroidered with a comet tail of multicolored hearts. In her haste to get to Paul, she stepped on the roller tray and it flipped, tossing white paint against the brand new purchase. Even when Paul spied the price tag—the shirt had cost forty-two dollars!—he simply said, "It's ok. Everything will come out fine." He was desperate to stop the tears, as well as the stare of Jess, unmoved at the door beside her Bloomingdale's bags.

"No, Daddy," Yanmei said, eyebrows wiggling with inspiration. "Actually, I think I am this full." She put a hand against her bangs as if in salute.

"Are you ready to explode?"

"Daddy, wait, wait!" She slid from the booth and lifted first one hand and then the other as far as she could above her head. "I am this this full!"

"How are we going to fit you in the car?"

Yanmei giggled. Her pinched eyes reminded Paul of the curved, dark shells of sunflower seeds he liked to crunch while watching the Phillies on slow-moving Saturday afternoons. What if he just slouched down in the booth, feet up on the seat cushion, and enjoyed his daughter's antics without the least thought of time? Theoretically, nothing could stop him; he was, after all, dining at an all-you-can-eat restaurant. To other customers, he might simply be relaxing between trips to the buffet. Maybe if they both kept just a little bit of food on their plates, the waitress would think they were still eating. Maybe the check would never come.

—⁂—

"I need her back by seven," Jess had announced that morning as Paul stood on a throw rug in the entryway of the huge, strange house, a vast sea of hand-laid tile swirling around him. His wife added the word "please" only after she'd returned from another room with Yanmei's jacket. "Please," she said in a tone so flat, so consciously neutral, that it was clear she was only being grudgingly polite.

"Mei wenti," he said, accepting the jacket—an obnoxious pink thing with a smiling, vaguely ethnic cartoon girl embroidered on the back.

"What does that mean?"

Now there was a distinct edge to her voice, and Paul looked closely at Jess for the first time since he arrived. It had been less than a week since he'd seen her, but he was startled by the change. Her long, pleasantly sloppy blonde hair had been cut away and shaped into the contour of a professional cycling helmet. Her cozy brown eyes were gone, covered up by brilliant green contact lenses that made her look strange—an extremely attractive but still alien being.

"Mei wenti," he repeated, shrugging, smiling, scratching an earlobe—too self-conscious to make any of these gestures seem natural. "No problem."

And it was true: Getting his daughter back on time wouldn't be the problem. That was simply a matter of calculating driving distances, determining the duration of activities, of keeping an eye on his watch. The real problem was that, for the past five days, Paul had been living alone in their brick twin in Chester while Jess and Yanmei had taken up residence in this five bedroom palace in Swarthmore. Ostensibly, his wife was housesitting for her employer, who'd breezed out of the country with her husband for a three-month cruise of the Mediterranean. In reality, this was nothing less than a trial separation.

Before things became too awkward, Yanmei bounded down the stairs. Such a strange sound, Paul thought, the hard, awkward knocking against the bare wood surface. It struck him as harsh and unfriendly compared to the soft drumming she made on the carpeted stairs at home.

"Where we going?" she cried, throwing herself at Paul's leg for a hug. He picked her up, putting her lovely plump face between his wife's and his own.

"It's a gimungous surprise," Paul said.

Yanmei let out a loud squeal.

"Do you have to be—?" Jess said, covering her ears.

She screamed a second time, turning down the volume a bit.

"That's not appropriate behavior."

"But Mommy," she said, turning in Paul's arms toward her, undaunted by that hard green glare. "I'm going to have a surprise!"

—⁜—

They'd driven to Center City to see *Journey to the West*, a puppet show at Painted Bride Theater. Paul had told Jess about his plans the previous night on the phone, at first diplomatically resisting her objections to doing anything "too Chinese." However, when she went on to admonish him by saying, "The name, the language, the activities—you keep emphasizing her difference, you'll only end up pushing her away," Paul had to interrupt, asking politely as possible, "Just how much more are you going to ask me to do?" That stopped the objections ("Whatever," she said, "it's your day with her"), but the disagreement had gnawed at him well into the next afternoon, as he and Yanmei watched black clad actors dance wide-eyed puppets around the stage. In one scene, Buddha buried the mischievous Monkey under a giant mountain. After the lights dimmed for a few dramatic moments, a screen above read, "Five Hundred Years Later," at which point a monk named Xuanzang appeared, searching for Monkey, whom the holy man needed to help retrieve the sacred scriptures from India. Monkey began to wiggle under the mountain and Xuanzang swooped over to pull and yank and—pop!—the puppet flew off the arm of the pirouetting actor and clattered like a skeleton across the stage. Paul could feel Yanmei shaking with laughter by his side. He wanted to enjoy the moment, but in the back of his mind he kept worrying about the tone he'd taken with Jess. Exactly how much further had his somewhat snide question pushed her toward a final, irrevocable break?

In the lobby after the show, Paul bought Yanmei two finger puppets, which she used to re-enact the moment of Monkey's escape. This performance drew the attention of a smiling, middle-aged couple who followed them out the door.

"Is she Oriental?" the man asked, adjusting narrow-framed glasses.

"She was born in China." Paul was used to such questions. Unlike Jess, who would oftentimes chastise people for their nosiness, he could not help but be polite.

"She speak English?"

"Ask me. I'm right down here," Yanmei said, waving a hand.

The couple laughed.

"We adopted her when she was eleven months old."

The woman tentatively put out a hand, as if she wanted to touch

Yanmei but was afraid she would bite. "How do you get . . . how much?" she asked.

"You're too old," Yanmei said.

The last thing Paul could bear was a scene. Quickly wishing the couple "goodbye," he nudged Yanmei down the street. Only when they turned the corner did he delicately attempt to reprimand her.

"But Daddy," she pouted. "I was just answering questions."

Which was true. One of the many things that Paul had come to love about Yanmei was her frankness—her utter lack of fear. He liked to think that this quality came from her biological mother. He knew nothing about the woman, but long ago, he'd created a story for himself about this Chinese family who had no money to pay the fine for their "extra" child. He imagined the mother sneaking from her house early one morning, singing to the tightly swaddled child on the long walk to a marketplace in Xiamen. She tried to appear calm, normal, but her eyes darted left and right; when she was sure no one was looking, she quickly deposited the girl in a crate by an unoccupied stall. Paul could almost see the woman's guilt-wracked walk back home—the quick steps, the fearful look behind before turning back to face the sun that was just beginning to peek out from the blanket edge of the horizon. He could see the baby resting blissfully in her container, maybe still an hour from being discovered by an old man slapping fresh fish onto a pile of ice. The woman who gave birth to her daughter—to Paul's daughter, his only child—maybe three weeks before, reached her dilapidated porch, pushed aside drying clothes hanging from a bamboo rod across the entrance and disappeared into shadows and silence of the house, only then feeling the full weight of what she'd done collapse upon her like a rain-rotted roof. Beyond that, Paul's imagination failed him, and perhaps it was just as well, for recently he had begun to experience a faint, gnawing suspicion that the woman in his story may have felt not only a deep loss but the bright spark of liberation as well.

"What would you like to eat?" he asked Yanmei to change the subject.

"Buf-ay, Buf-ay!" she said, clapping her hands.

The thought of how she said that word cheered Paul up for most of the thirty-minute drive from Center City to the restaurant just over the state line in Delaware, where his daughter scooted around the steam tables taking spoonfuls of this and that while Paul, eating well but without appetite, clung desperately to the notion that they could keep going up for more and in that way stretch the afternoon into forever. When that proved impracticable, Paul dragged himself to his feet, said "xie xie" and "zaijian" to the tired, unimpressed cashier who silently handed him his change, and ushered Yanmei out the door into the bright but slumping sun.

—m—

Years ago, the day after they'd submitted their formal application to the adoption agency, Jess had come home cradling a box of language CDs, exclaiming, "Ni hao ma? Let's learn Mandarin!"

Paul looked up from the third inning of a Phillies game. "Mandarin?"

"Chinese," she said.

"The language?"

"Of course." The response sounded less like an answer than an admonishment.

Together, they listened to the first three lessons on the CD. They read vocabulary words aloud. They studied flashcards of high frequency characters. There was a real energy to Jess's efforts, and Paul, who had seen her emotionally up and down for the last two years or so, went along for the ride. However, a few weeks later, while they were going over a lesson in bed, Jess suddenly tossed the workbook across the room. It struck the wall and fell to the floor, like a bee stung by a swatter.

"You know," she said. "I could really use an alphabet."

"It'll get easier," Paul offered.

"Oh reeeally?" she said, not even looking at him. "And who made you the expert?"

Paul didn't say a word; the last thing he wanted was an argument.

The following evening, Jess was on the phone with her sister—not Alison, the bubbly mother of three, but Lisa, the wild one, the sophomore at Villanova. Despite the years between them, they'd started, in the last few months or so, having long, occasionally uproarious conversations, as if they were best friends. Paul had come down the stairs that night just in time to hear Jess complaining that, "Chinese has too many tones." He looked at the flashcards in his hands. The top card appeared to be the silhouette of a terribly complicated building; he had no idea what the character meant. "Well," she continued, "take the word 'wu.' Wu in the third tone means 'five,' but in the fourth tone it means 'error.'" She laughed, but there was palpable anger behind it. "How can you even communicate like that?"

In the end, Jess gave up studying the language because she was "adopting a baby, not earning a degree." Paul struggled through three more lessons on his own before shelving the CDs for good. All these years later, the box was still in the living room on a shelf with their videos, the word CHINESE in bold red letters pointing toward the ceiling like some kind of an indoor lightning rod.

On the way home, while Yanmei's puppets debated the merits of a trip west for enlightenment, Paul thought about the long journey he'd taken together with his wife. Their relationship went all the way back to his adolescence—the summer after high school graduation, when on a day trip with friends to Wildwood he'd seen Jess leaving a boardwalk stand with a cup of water ice. She'd shot him an appraising glance and moved the bottom of her pink bikini for about ten or twelve paces before turning around for a wink.

In the early weeks of dating, Paul did everything he could to impress her. Fortunately, because of his work ethic and excellent customer service skills, he'd been promoted from the stockroom to the sales floor of the appliance store he'd started working at only a few months before. Good money was rolling in. With his new car—a four year old Escort—he was easily able to drive the half hour from Chester to her home in Haddonfield. He had no problem paying the toll to drive back over the Barry Bridge, no problem battling traffic on 202 in order to use his brand new credit card to buy Jess clothes from high-end stores at the King of Prussia Mall. He took her to fancy restaurants in Center City, where he made a show of paying for valet parking. As September approached, Paul put aside his plans to attend Delco Community College in order to devote his full energy to building this relationship with Jess.

Four months later, after a special Christmas dinner at a Main Line bistro, Jess climbed onto him in his car, beeping the horn with her behind to add some ceremony to the announcement that she would not be returning to school in the spring because she'd found a really good job as a receptionist in a doctor's office close to her home.

"Are you sure?" Paul asked.

"Believe me. It's pre-med enough for now."

"You should follow your dreams."

"I love," she said, giving him a hard garlic shrimp kiss on the lips, "absolutely everything you do for me."

Paul was so preoccupied with these thoughts that he failed to notice a compact truck roar up on his side and slice in front of him.

"Crazy," he muttered, shaking his head as he followed the vehicle—a Brinks truck—off I 95 and up the curving ramp to the Blue Route. On the back door was a sticker that said, STAY BACK.

"Daddy," Yanmei called from the backseat, "why don't you go fast sometimes?"

"Well, it's dangerous."

"But everybody's really moving."

"Does that mean I should too?"

"I'm wondering," she said after a lengthy pause, "exactly how many people are dangerous?"

It didn't take Paul long to apply this question to Jess, who had admitted on the phone the night before that she was "taking one hell of a gamble." The longer the separation continued, the greater the possibility that she could lose her husband, her only child, her house, the respect of her mother and father and Alison (Wild Lisa, if and when she found out the truth, would probably just say, "Cool!"). Jess would still have her job as a receptionist, but that wouldn't be enough to keep her in school, much less cover rent at wherever she'd have to go once this house-sitting escapade was over.

What was this if not the epitome of "dangerous"? To Paul, the point of life was to start early with something—a good, clear sense of the kind of world you wanted—and carefully and deliberately add to it as the years went by. It did not make sense to him to live half a life a certain way and then just wipe it out, like Yanmei at Ocean City when she was three and gleefully stomped all over the sandcastles it had taken them an hour to build. That's what little kids did; that was funny and fine. Mature adults were supposed to build strong, secure worlds and maintain them—let them stand for good.

Even since Yanmei came home with them, however, Jess had been troubling the edifice. Initially, Paul chalked it up to post-adoption depression, which their social worker had warned them about. However, the protracted periods of brooding continued without relief. She sought more and more time alone. Paul was concerned, but he did what he thought best—he gave her space, and Jess used that space to flit around, eager and unfocused, to different activities: a reading club for three months, yoga for a half a year, a second job at a coffee shop one evening a week, an introductory biology course at Delco. Then, after a surprisingly sunny period of time at home, during which she threw herself into ambitious arts and crafts projects with Yanmei, Jess enrolled in college full time. Despite the scheduling adjustments, despite the financial burden of both school and part-time day care, they had avoided quarrelling. Given the incessant pyrotechnics of his parents and the seething silences of her mom and dad, this was something of which, regardless of the sacrifice, Paul was especially proud.

One night—a Tuesday, at 8:32 p.m., not long after Paul had come downstairs from putting Yanmei to bed—Jess came into the kitchen with a bottle of spring water and laid out her plans in cold, clear English. Periodically, she'd pause to sip from the bottle and then screw back on the cap. As he listened, Paul picked at a slice of sticky kuchen on a napkin in front of him.

"No more goofing around," she said. "I've got to make a meaningful move."

He said he understood only because he didn't know what to say.

"I'm not being unreasonable," she said.

It wasn't a defense—there was no guilt or remorse in her voice. It was an announcement, spoken in a tone that forestalled all objection.

"I am going to live at this other place for a while. Yanmei will stay with me because my schedule is more flexible. We can arrange times for you to see her."

Paul listened to the cap being unscrewed from the bottle, the slosh of the water, the suck of the sip.

"Daddy, are you dangerous?" Yanmei asked.

The day after she'd moved out, Jess called to say, "I'm a terrible person," to which he said, "No, no you're not. Please don't say that."

"I'm trying to find my way."

"I can help," he said.

There was a pause. Paul wondered if Jess were busy unscrewing a bottle cap or something.

"No," she said. "You can't."

"Why?"

"Because whether you realize it or not, you'd be leading me, leading me in the direction you want me to go."

"Just tell me," he said. "Is there someone else?"

Paul had expected her to take a few moments to think of a tactful way to break him the news, but she responded immediately—with vehemence. "Are you serious?"

He nodded into the phone.

"I love you Paul." There was a pause, and he wanted to fill it up with a similar declaration, but the question "why?" kept breaking up the words he tried to form.

"I love you so much," she said, this time with deep feeling. He could tell that she was crying. "But, you know . . . I love me too."

Somehow, Paul had closed the distance between his car and the Brinks truck. "STAY BACK," the sticker continued to command.

"Daddy, can you please answer a question?"

He let off the gas, and the vehicle pulled away. In a moment or two, it was the size of a fist, gone off to bully someone else for a while.

—⁂—

At the magnificent house in Swarthmore, sitting on a hard backed chair in the living room and gazing into the empty fireplace, Paul couldn't help but think how comfortable—how "at home"—Jess seemed to be. She sat on the black leather sofa with a casual elegance, one long leg across the cushions and the other tucked underneath her behind. Yanmei was upstairs going to the bathroom. On the coffee table was an attractive local celebrity turned restaurateur on the cover of *Main Line Today.*

Finally, because he had no other recourse, he looked up at Jess. She shifted on the sofa. She looked at him for a moment before her green eyes escaped to the ceiling. "I don't hear you flushing," she said.

"Mommy, I'm NOT DONE yet!"

Jess slapped her knees. Turning to Paul, she said, "I should give you a tour."

Paul had no idea why she would say such a thing or why he would choose to follow her when she rose from the couch and walked into the dining room, but he did. He listened as she described the thrilling features of the house: the French doors in the kitchen opening up into a meticulously sculpted garden, complete with pebbled walkways and a screened-in gazebo; the gorgeous half-moon window in the dining room; the immaculate hardwood floors; an intricately patterned Persian rug under an antique dining room table that, as Jess proudly announced, "must have cost a fortune"; the cherry cabinets in the kitchen; the stainless steel side-by-side refrigerator with a TV and DVD player.

"I sold one of these the other day," Paul said, caressing the smooth, shiny door of the appliance.

"Really?"

It was difficult to gauge her tone. Was she taking interest? Simply being polite? Subtly mocking him? "Yes," he said. "These babies are well made. Not cheap. Heavy as hell."

At the end of the tour, Paul half-expected his wife to give him her card. Instead, she just shrugged and glanced at him before casting eyes back at the ceiling. It occurred to him that she might be waiting for him to make a move—to give some definitive sign of just how much he loved her. Even were he the type of man to take the initiative—to maybe grab his wife by the shoulders and reclaim her with a powerful, passionate kiss—he had a hunch that would be just about the worst thing he could do.

There was Yanmei at last, thank God—the awkward clumping down those uncovered stairs. She was coming down to thank him, to hug him, to kiss him. She was coming to say goodbye.

"Daddy, I was wondering," Yanmei said, "Is five hundred years a long time?"

"Yes."

"Did Monkey get scared?"

"I don't think so."

"Did he get lonely?"

"Maybe. Probably. I don't know."

Paul grimaced. Yanmei frowned. Patting her stylish, aerodynamic hair, Jess looked like the cover of next month's *Main Line Today*.

—⁂—

Even though it was an early Saturday evening, there was inexplicable stop-and-go traffic on the Blue Route. As Paul inched along, he again had difficulty breathing. There was no way out. It was like that interminable plane ride home from China: fourteen harrowing hours from Guangzhou to Newark, more than half a day inside that long, terrible tube with no sense of progress until the pilot spoke over the intercom to tell them where they were. He looked down at the baby—his daughter—fussing in the extra seat they'd purchased and tried to will her to be quiet. When that didn't work, he walked the aisles, bouncing her up and down to stop the crying, whispering "bie ku" ("don't cry"). Up and down he went, with nowhere else to go except into his mind, which had been filling since take off with doubts about whether he could be a parent, whether he could handle the grueling day-to-day, whether he could bleed that long and that deeply with love.

—⁂—

When he finally arrived home, he tossed his keys on the table just to make some noise. He went to the phone on the kitchen counter; in the dark window of the answering machine was a bright red 0—the same story as this morning.

He opened the fridge, basking in its cold glow for a few pleasant moments before grabbing a beer. He called his friend Scott and left a message. In an hour or so, the Sixers would be on. Iverson was gone and the team had been mathematically eliminated from the playoffs, but still, maybe Scott would call and they could meet at Tom and Jerry's to watch them do their best against the Spurs.

Paul sat on the couch doing nothing for a full five minutes. He got up and drank another beer while rereading the junk mail. He paged through a book of coupons, cutting out a few and putting them in the box where Jess kept them organized. Over a third beer, he watched a travel show on PBS. He went upstairs to go to the bathroom, taking comfort in the sound of his feet on the floor. He stood at the sink and made a mental list of places he wanted to take his daughter next week, and the week after that. She was old enough now for the art museum. Then there was the Please Touch Museum, the Franklin Institute, the aquarium in Camden. It was a big city: they would not soon run out of things to do.

Paul went back into the hallway. The door to Yanmei's room was closed—a good thing. He went into the office to find the computer just sitting there—no blinking modem light, no comforting hum of the fan. The blank monitor looked at him with indifference. He could boot up and surf a bit, click "refresh" on the *Times* front page to maybe see a different picture or a story filed just a minute ago and in that way give himself the illusion that something alive was with him in the room. This, however, seemed an awful way to spend the evening.

Frustrated, anxious, he went back down the stairs, struck them hard, the boom of tennis shoes against carpet a muffled song until he hit the living room floor and stood still, at which point the silence squeezed in on him from everywhere. It's not so bad, it's not so bad, he chanted to himself over and over again until he recovered. Still, he needed something—anything—to do to survive the silence. He looked around the dimly lit room and spied the box of language CDs on the bookshelf. Next to it was a folder of exercises he'd long ago printed out from the Internet. Paul took the folder over to the dining room table, sat down, and pulled out a blank character worksheet. There was a particular stroke order, which he didn't remember, and that made him want to find something else to do. He resisted the impulse. He was going to do this; he was going to follow through. One of Yanmei's colored pencils was stuck like a sword into the scented candle on the table. He pulled it out and, on impulse, held it to his lips. He started writing some easy characters: a horizontal line for the number one, two lines for two, a simple cross for ten. Then he got down to serious work, drawing a comma in reverse, a tiny "l," a pair of marks like flattened periods, a simple "x". He drew vertical lines and horizontal slashes, cute, miniature boxes and something close to a high heeled shoe. "Mei Wenti. Mei Wenti. Mei Wenti," he wrote—three syllables, three times, the third set still shaky, but without doubt the sturdiest of them all.

Search

Groggie's was a rather grim place to end a campus interview, but it was the only place outside of the cafeteria that served food, or what passed for it. I held the door for Ms. Dunbar, and we stepped inside, shoes squishing beer-soaked carpet. Overhead was a poker match, a row of hearts bunched in the corner of the screen. It would be an hour until students stumbled in, licking lips for Hump Day specials.

The interview was officially over, and Ms. Dunbar, our applicant, had an early evening flight back to Ohio. Dennis, our considerate chair, suggested I take her out for something—the academic equivalent of a game show's "lovely parting gifts."

"Or," I said to her, thinking of my own obligations for the evening, "I could just drop you at the airport. Give you some time for yourself."

"No, no," Ms. Dunbar said, eyes fearless for the first time all visit. "I could really use a drink."

I laughed, and she smiled, hoping, I suppose, that this human moment might be taken into account when my colleagues met to deliberate.

We scanned sticky plastic menus. Except for the side salad, everything was fried. "Anything you like?" I asked.

"The chicken fingers look good."

Had the interview been a success, she would have been laughing uproariously with the entire department at some microbrewery in a nice part of town. She had to have known this. To her credit, Ms. Dunbar was a good sport. She was well into her thirties, and her brave face fit her like a glove.

A boy with vaguely familiar sideburns shuffled to our table. I ordered the basket of fingers and two gin and tonics.

"Were you one of my students?" I asked. He looked to me like the whimsical personification of an F.

"Maybe," the boy said, scratching an armpit. "Oceanography? I remember the Bluntnose Shiner."

"I specialize in Renaissance literature."

He laughed. "Right. That's what I was thinking of."

The boy left, and I watched Ms. Dunbar study the hanging jerseys, the framed NASCAR posters, the infamous scrawl wall upon which students poured out their hearts, as long as they kept it clean. I was not good at small talk, especially after the morning coffee wore off.

"Your students asked such thoughtful questions," she said.

"I'm glad you thought so."

Ms. Dunbar's teaching demonstration had been a disappointment. Her curriculum vitae boasted a wealth of teaching experience—large and small school, private and public, rural and urban. She had strong recommendations as well. However, Eyler, our surly Postmodernist, had "grave concerns" about her research. "Longfellow!" he'd cried more than once during our fall deliberations. "Longfellow!"—each time the author's name shot from his mouth with the surprise of a sneeze. The others had reservations as well, but in a narrow vote, it was agreed that she should be one of the three to bring to campus.

At the beginning of her demonstration, Ms. Dunbar rubbed hands excitedly and said, "Today, I'm going to talk to you about a poem called 'Paul Revere's Ride.' " Next to me, Eyler dug a pen cap into his palms. Michael, our Norris scholar, fumed like Marcus at McTeague. Oblivious, Ms. Dunbar paced the room reading the poem, one stanza per row until she finished. To make matters worse, she just talked and talked. "Such a good husband," she said of the poet. "Such a good man." Then: awkward silence. Ms. Dunbar stood in front of us, anthology like a dead song bird in her hands, mouth moving fruitlessly, until Jillian Wycoff, one of our best, asked if she would like a cup of water. In Ms. Dunbar's mind, Jillian must have been who she meant by all those "thoughtful" students.

The boy with the sideburns brought our drinks, and we spent the next few minutes sighing and taking sips. I asked her about Ohio, and she said the town where she lived was small and more than a bit desperate around the edges. As a city girl, she could never get used to how dark the night became. "You look up," she said, "and if the stars aren't there it's like you've ceased to exist." I suspected she was alone—and that she was one of the many women of her age who thought there was a criminal for this crime.

My cell phone rang, which seemed a mercy until I saw it was my wife.

"I don't care, really," I said, trying to keep my voice level. That evening, we had a dinner engagement in Center City—old acquaintances from graduate school who were breezing through to see their youngest son, an Ancient History major at Penn. Sandy, the once-skittish graduate student I'd nursed through his dissertation, was retired already. His wife had come into serious money, and he had been annoyingly wise with his own. In short, I wasn't keen on seeing them. My wife, however, seemed to think this was the opportunity of a lifetime and had been calling every hour with a new idea for a restaurant: White Dog, Queen of Sheba. Alma de Cuba. "Pick and be done with it," I said.

Our order arrived in a plastic basket. The fingers—five of them—were dark, gnarled, and hard. We both blinked at the food in silent dismay. Finally, I took a healthy bite of one to prove that they were edible. Ms. Dunbar nibbled another and wiped her fingers on a cocktail napkin.

We ate in silence. I thought to ask if she needed ketchup, but she said she was fine. More silence. She made a comment about the poker on the TV screen, and I said, "You gotta know when to fold them," instantly regretting it, of course, because she was sure to understand it as some cryptic comment about her professional fate. I switched to the subject of Ohio, forgetting I'd asked about it only minutes before.

"Oh, it's become a kind of home," she said. There were the small pleasures: the sprawling farmer's market, the artsy shops on Court Street, a misty morning jog along the Hocking.

"I used to run," I said.

"Really? Why did you stop?"

I put hand to heart and made an ugly face. To my surprise, Ms. Dunbar dropped her head. My eyes were left to wander a white scar-like path of scalp. After a few moments, I asked,

"Do you need—?"

"I'm sorry," she said, eyes shimmering. "I, it's just that . . . it's been a really long day."

I glanced at my watch. It had been a long day—seemed like years ago already since Ms. Dunbar finished her demonstration, years since she'd been escorted by Jillian to the art gallery for the last stop on her itinerary and I dared to think there might be time for a brief nap before my dinner engagement. Eyler, though, his eyes blazing, hustled everyone into the nearest empty classroom, slammed shut the door, and declared, "No way in hell!"

"There's no reason for swearing," Donna said, rattling her bangles.

"She's someone I could see myself working with," Dennis said.

Eyler stared at him. He gave the applicant's CV a squeeze.

Julia said, "Was one lousy drink going to hurt her?" At the dinner the night before, Ms. Dunbar had ordered a Diet Coke. Scowling, Julia ordered a third martini just to make a point.

"Look," Michael said. "From the beginning, I didn't like those two blank years—out of the loop for 'personal reasons.' Did anyone press her on this?"

"I hate personal reasons," Eyler said.

Michael smiled. He started check marking the document in front of him. "And after that, one year appointments here and there. Some of you call this experience. I call it desperation. Longfellow or not, she's stale bread and it shows."

Eyler crossed his arms and grinned at Donna. "A-the hell-men," he said.

—⁂—

On the way to the airport, I became loquacious. Maybe it was the gin or maybe it was just my natural passion for the subject, but when Ms. Dunbar asked about my research, I told her all about Walter Raleigh: the failure at Roanoke, those years in The Tower of London, the vain quest for El Dorado. As we pulled up to her terminal, I thought it fitting to end the lecture with a little of his verse. "Stab at thee he that will," I declared in my most emotionally affecting voice,

"No stab thy soul can kill." I glanced over to gauge the effect of these comforting words. Ms. Dunbar was staring through the windshield, eyes shiny with tears.

When we got out of the car, things became more awkward still. Ms. Dunbar dragged her suitcase from the trunk and tugged at the handle, which refused to budge. "This happens sometimes," she said before kicking the bag savagely to the ground. She picked it up and yanked again; this time, the handle shot out with such force that the leather purse on her shoulder slipped to the crotch of her arm. An electronic device clattered to the pavement.

When she gathered herself, I stuck out my hand and said, "Ms. Dunbar, it's been a real pleasure."

"Maybe I should have lectured on 'The Cross of Snow.'"

I nodded, as if I understood.

"Thing is, I know I wouldn't have made it past line two."

"You'll hear from us in a week," I said, smiling with all the teeth I could manage. "If not sooner."

—⁂—

Later that night, I sat in my home office, door locked, staring into the fireplace glow of the computer screen. Dinner had gone about as badly as expected. Sandy held forth, of course, and my wife, as she'd done for thirty-two years, took up the conversational slack. I drank glass after glass of wine so that, come dessert, I could angrily wonder aloud: "Isn't retirement a bore? How can you stand to sit around the house all day?"

"It's paradise," Sandy said with a hearty laugh. "What comes next is the problem!"

"Stop it," his wife said. "He had one of those scares . . ."

"They saw something on the MRI." He took a bite of his Death by Chocolate. "A shadow."

"Oh," his wife said, slapping him lightly on the arm, "turns out it was just his big fat ego!"

We all laughed; Sandy, a successful career tucked like a child into bed, laughed the loudest of us all. Suddenly, he took his wife's hand and brought it to his heart. "What would she do without me?" he said, blinking away tears. Embarrassed, I studied the wine spots on the tablecloth.

On the keyboard lay Ms. Dunbar's CV which I'd forgotten to bring with me this morning. Such nice, substantial paper. Such a clean, no-nonsense font. Such concise descriptions of every move of her professional life. I'd been over it several times in the last three months, and there was not a single word or piece of punctuation out of place.

It was 10:15. She'd be getting back to Ohio just about now, and I imagined her pushing open a warped door to cramped, roach-ruined rooms. A tabby cat would run against her leg. There'd be a coffee table—plywood over books—and an unmade futon in the bedroom, where she'd sit night after night to wring her hands and wait for our call.

After a quick search, I found Ms. Dunbar's Facebook page. Her last post, a giddy "Cannot believe my luck!!!" from two weeks ago, had yielded just a single response: "'I will never fail you or forsake you'"—this from a woman I supposed to be her mother.

I heard my wife in the bathroom—water from the faucet, the tap of toothbrush against sink. The toilet flushed. I couldn't hire Ms. Dunbar, but I could send a message—a show of empathy to make up for the awkwardness of that afternoon. The cursor blinked patiently in the subject box while I tried to think of the best way to begin. At last, I typed out "Ms. Dunbar," then fixed it to "Gwen." I decided to finish my lecture on Raleigh, focus on the message of his demise. August, 1618, the Palace of Westminster. An old, ailing man, long out of favor with the king, the poet pledged allegiance to James for half an hour before the crowd that had come to see him die. Then, in one deft stroke, the head came off and was sent to be embalmed. "Often", I typed more earnestly now, "I'm moved close to tears by the thought of those sealed lids, the sewn up mouth, the cleansed face radiant with repose. Gwen, you may well find it a comfort to know the story of what happened then: The next morning bright, London pungent with life, Elizabeth arrived at court to claim her husband's head and, true love knowing no bounds, kept it close in a sack for the rest of her earth-bound days."

Red Right 88

THE EYES ARE slits, but Ray thuds through a chuckhole on the bridge over the Metroparks Zoo, and Eli, his ceaselessly scrambling two year old, comes to life again, lifting his wispy-haired head from the car seat to blink at the passing world. Ray holds his breath, steps on the gas to make it through a yellow light. Keep moving, keep moving— nice and steady. Moments later, the boy nestles back on the car seat, and his lids begin to flutter. After another few blocks, they close, and his mouth springs open like a poorly wrapped Christmas gift. He is, thank the newborn Jesus, asleep at last.

Ray waits two minutes before turning on the radio: Santa stuff, soporific rock, sports talk kicking off.

"Look," a gruff voice bellows. "I love our Cleveland Browns, but I'm not naïve. I'm aware of the cold, hard facts: 1) the team is a pitiful 5-10, 2) they haven't had a franchise QB since Bernie, and 3) they've blown for years louder and harder than The Judgment Day All-Star Band."

Ray smiles. There was a time he had such interest—such passion.

"BUUUUUT—and this, I grant you, is a BUUUUUT of epic proportions—say there was, I don't know, a genie out there, a football genie, and he gave you one wish, a do-over . . . if, in other words, this supernatural fella had the power to make good on your request to change one single thing that has happened to this poor, God-forsaken franchise since 1964—"

"Red Right 88," Ray says aloud, tapping the wheel, a brilliant game show contestant who doesn't need the rest of the question. Although he hasn't lived in this city now for years, the fateful play looms large in his imagination: January, 1981, the divisional playoffs, late in the frozen fourth quarter and the Browns, involved in so many close, heart-pounding games throughout that unforgettable year, are down by two. Ray is seven and watching the game with his father and Uncle Ben, each with handfuls of hair in his hands. He squeezes a Kardiac Brick, a chunk of red foam that's been hurled at the TV more than once this afternoon, while Brian Sipe—Cleveland's All-Pro quarterback, the handsome transplant from sunny San Diego—takes the snap, peddles back in the pocket, plants his left foot in the turf, and floats a loose spiral through sub-zero air into the cradle-like arms of an Oakland Raider whose name Ray refuses to recall. In his clean and simple do-over world, Rutigliano would send out the field goal unit so Cockroft, shaky all afternoon in lake effect wind and snow, could Super Toe it through the uprights for the dramatic one-point win.

"Think about it folks," the host says. "Go back and root around in the dark and dusty corners of your mind. Shine a light on the painful stuff. Release the ghosts that haunt you to this very day. Zelonka will be here for you all the way til four, at which point, Merry Christmas!—you guys'll be on your own."

Ray is on his own right now, and to him this time is more delicious than a wedge of Aunt Karen's sweet potato pie, fresh from the oven. Now that Eli's out, how much better is it to be behind the wheel of his Prius than back at his parents' house, with the exhaust of pre-party anxiety poisoning the air. How much better than this morning, during the mad hustle to get ready for mass, when Ray, wanting simply to brush his teeth, eased open the bathroom door to discover Dorie in underpants and bra, hands in the air, stomach like a ball on the inside corner. "Ahhgg!" she cried, "Why don't you do something!" while Eli kicked off the toilet seat and screamed, "doan wah ta, doan wah ta, doan wah ta!" Ray returned to the bedroom and lay down in his best shirt and tie, hearing despite the pillows over his face his son's escalating screams. On and on the boy went, while Ray, imagining what their next child might add to the mix, began to drown in a gravy boat worth of misgivings. At what point in his mind had his wife's panties become mere underpants? When had they made what seemed to him a conscious decision to hang so sadly from her behind?

"On the other side of break," Zelonka says, "we're going to hear from Thom, The WhamBammer, J.T., and, let's see, batting cleanup, the always entertaining Dawg Pound Dougie!"

Ray glances in the rearview mirror. Eli's lips are thick with drool, his face soft and surprisingly jowly. Deep, gorgeous sleep—the boy is good for at least two hours. By the time Ray returns home, maybe the stuffed pork loin will be under control and his parents will be speaking to each other again. Maybe Dorie, who's burdened herself with a side dish complicated as a blitz scheme by Dick LeBeau, will flash him the kind of smile that is not a blade to the throat. If nothing else, maybe Uncle Ben will have arrived to officially open the liquor table for business.

A car commercial shouts—"Act now before all the best deals are gone!"—and Ray finds himself replaying that ill-fated pass again and again in his mind: the drop back, the bounce, the step forward, the release. When, he wonders, was the precise moment that Sipe regretted his choice? When did the thought, "I can squeeze this baby in to Ozzie" become "I've just made what will become the biggest mistake of all my football days"?

Openings. Opportunities. Decisions. Game-changing mistakes. The words sling him right back to his parents, who've been worse than ever this holiday season: the carefully controlled nitpicking; the sly, adversarial looks across the dining room table, the wind-chilled silences that have the last two nights driven Ray and Dorie to bed at the earliest reasonable time. Once—he places the memory early, not too long after that fateful playoff game—his father with index finger and thumb explained that he and Ray's mother had always been "a degree apart," which sounded close enough. But a degree, Ray came to understand, was not the difference between 1 and 0 on a January afternoon. No, it was the difference of four full years—the difference between a human resources manager for a marketing firm and an automotive technician at a neighborhood mom and pop shop. It was, in the end, the difference between young, passionate love and middle-aged making the best of what you have.

The sports show returns, and Ray, left and righting his new car on a whim, takes perverse pleasure in losing himself in the nightmares these callers recount: Red Right 88 (of course), The Drive, The Fumble, The Move, The Draft (1999-present). Ray tries to resist, but he can't help it—he feels that old game-day tug toward total strangers with whom he shares nothing but the ardent desire to one day see the home team roll in convertibles down Euclid for a victory parade.

When WhamBammer gets on the line, he says, "Zel, I've got two simple words for you: 'The Shot.'"

"We're talking football, man," Zelonka cries. "We open it up to every sport, we'll be here til the cows come home!"

"Come on, you can't tell me that one wasn't a killer."

"Seriously? Michael Jordan over Ehlo? Craig Ehlo? You're going to cry in your cranberries about that? Tell me you couldn't see that one coming . . ."

—⁂—

Ray is not conscious of where he is until a tight spiral of pain burrows into his chest. To his left is an old strip mall—dour and spiritless but achingly familiar. There's the bowling alley, the Chinese restaurant, the absurdly resilient Radio Shack. Anna, Ray thinks, Anna Viviani. She worked at a shoe store right here at the corner, and many years ago (he won't do the sad, simple math), Ray stopped in with his good friend Mark Mijovic to buy a pair of Air Jordans, and Anna, dressed charmingly like a referee, said with bright eyes and a blithe wave of the hand, "I'd love to take the next person in line!" At the counter, Ray glanced at the girl's name tag and saw a lovely collarbone. He was an eighteen-year-old boy and had of course come to notice many appealing things about the opposite sex—the color of eyes, the contour of lips, the curve of breasts inside form-fitting tops—but this was the first time he thought of a collarbone as something other than what might be snapped in two during a gang tackle at a Turkey Bowl game with his friends. When she handed him the receipt, their fingers accidentally touched. She smiled—she had an all-pro smile. Afterward, he slouched in Mark's Chevette, a huge plastic bag crackling like a fire between his legs.

"'Please come again,'" Mark said with a laugh. "What else could that mean but she wants you bad?"

Ray squinted at the tinted storefront window. He could see no sign of the girl that had reduced him to a fumbling mess. Had she returned to the register distracted, reliving the thrilling shock of his inadvertent finger against hers while she tried to sweet talk some squawking old lady out of her complaint? Had he already been supplanted by a better looking guy, one suave enough to take all her sunny interest in stride?

Mark sighed. "Go back in. Ask her out."

Ray gripped and released the plastic bag—rehab after an awful collision.

"Oh Christ, I'll do it for you."

Mark jumped from the car, threw the door closed against Ray's protests, and marched back into the store. To beat back panic, Ray closed his eyes and held his breath. A minute later, there was a pounding at his window, and when he opened his eyes he saw Mark waving a candystriped banner of receipt tape at his face. Looking closer, he saw a series of numbers in leprechaun green. Seven of them. Lucky all around. Back in the car, Mark said, "You'll be pleased to know I did not have to beg!" Ray looked away, afraid he might burst into tears.

Ray turns now into this old familiar parking lot for a closer look and discovers that the shoe store is now a pawn shop. In the window, WE BUY GOLD! and INSTANT CASH! are scrawled in a gaudy, used car lot font. It's Christmas, so of course the lights are off. This is a small mercy, although it can't keep him from imagining the sacrilege of some squat, bedraggled guy at that same counter offering three-second appraisals of class rings, baseball cards, and whatever other mementos the neighborhood's desperate souls have to sell.

—⁂—

On the night of their first date, Anna had to stay late to close. Ray arrived ten minutes early at the store, self-conscious in his father's colossal Crown Vic. He tried to build up his nerve with heavy metal—Scorpions, Blue Öyster Cult—but the music only made him more anxious. While he was rummaging through the glove box for something more sophisticated, Anna appeared in the supernal glow of a parking lot lamp—tall, slim, more beautiful than he remembered. He watched her lock up, readjust the heart-sized purse upon her shoulder, and approach with an easy stride. The door sprung open, and there she was—the hypnotic smell of vanilla and strawberry gum; curving lips around immaculate teeth; thin fingers upon the upholstery as she moved one long summer leg after the other onto the seat.

At a fast food restaurant the next day, Ray tried to describe to Mark his initial response to Anna's proximity, using the metaphor of last year's Turkey Bowl, when Moose Mauer kneed him in the gut as he stretched for a bad pass over the middle. Ray writhed on the gooshy earth, ripping at pale tufts of grass while his buddies chuckled above him. For a long terrifying time, breath would not come, it would not come, and then—thank God—it did.

"I'm embarrassed for you," his friend said, splintering a taco shell with his teeth, beef and cheese going all over the place. Ray cleared his throat to defend himself, but Mark turned to the window, unable to stomach the next indignity bound to sail out of Ray's mouth.

Ray couldn't help himself; he was in love. "I think she is the one."

"The one? The one what?"

"You know, the one I'm supposed to be with."

"There's only one? In the whole world? And she just happens to live in Cleveland—a mile from your home?"

"Mark, it's destiny! If you had a soul, a heart . . ."

Mark pinched taco filling between fingers and thumb and threw it in his mouth. "Believe me, a functional brain is more than enough."

—⁂—

The car rattles suddenly, and Ray's head snaps. He glances in the rearview mirror, as if the sight of the chuckhole he just struck will retroactively save him from the shock.

Eli, meanwhile, blissfully sleeps on.

—⁂—

For a good portion of his youth, Ray had been a person to whom most things came easily: school, sports, friends, girls. As he grew older and witnessed the struggles of others—chronic illness, rampant acne, social awkwardness, sluggishness of mind—he did not, like some cruel boys he knew, conclude he was some higher order of being. Instead, he began to worry something might be terribly wrong. Why, as a nine year old, was he such a whiz with fractions and decimals? Why, as a twelve year old, was he able to cleanly field a grounder in the hole and make that quick, accurate throw to first? Why, well into his first year of adolescence, had he never been sick for more than a day or two of his life? Why, in short, had he been given so many gifts when so many others had few to none? More importantly, when was his long, good run going to end?

By seventh grade, Ray became subject to brief periods of dread that seeped into him like water through the cracked soles of shoes. After a time, as his good fortune persisted, he'd dry out, metaphorically speaking, and return to his good, sunny self once again. But whatever stage in the cycle he found himself, he made sure to be always a model Christian. Because he was a sports star—because his saintly ways relieved them of the onerous duty to be good themselves—his classmates spared him their mockery.

Ray's charmed life came to an end when Mrs. Salinas, his eighth grade teacher, assigned a research report on the theme of "Desert Island Dreams." She had the children draw up a list of the top five things they could absolutely not live without and then pick one to talk about in front of the entire class. Baseball was the one obsession that had driven his young life. Tee ball, Little League, and now Junior League—he'd always been a force at the plate and in the field.

Although he'd never make it to Williamsport (Brian Sipe did—in fact, his team won the Little League World Series in '61), he had every reason to believe that within a few years he'd be playing varsity ball at whatever private high school was lucky enough to have him. A Division I scholarship would follow, and a few years later he'd be in the Major Leagues, the next Ripken or Smith or—if fate could spare him nothing more—Felix Fermin.

Because baseball was too broad of a topic for the report, Ray zeroed in on his beloved Indians, even though his hometown team did little year after year to inspire his continued devotion. He knew they'd won the Series back in 1948 (his grandfather had been at Game Four and had a Kenny Keltner foul ball to prove it), but he'd no idea that the team had won another championship twenty-eight years before.

In the school library, sitting behind a stack of Mark's books about chameleons, Ray read from an encyclopedia the unbelievable news that he had a sporting namesake—Ray Chapman, a do-everything shortstop who was just coming into his prime for the Indians in 1920. A paragraph later, he discovered the appalling news that in August of that year, during the team's exciting pennant run, this same

Ray Chapman, a batter who loved to crowd the plate, was killed by a fastball to the skull. Of all things, a New York Yankee fastball. He was only twenty-nine.

"Why didn't you tell me?" Ray cried, bursting through the front door after school.

Mom, still in crisp work clothes, looked up with managerial eyes from a box of microwave chicken. She'd never been a great fan of garish displays of emotion.

"My name, my name! Why, why, why?"

Mom's rationale had been quite simple: "Ray" for "ray of sunshine." It was a poetic turn of which she hardly seemed capable. When he told her what he'd learned, she shrugged. "Sorry dear, I honestly did not know."

But Dad—a huge sports fan, a lifelong gamer—had known. "What's the big deal?" he said, reaching into the fridge for his after-work Coors. "By all accounts, he was a damn fine player."

"Please don't use obscenities in front of the child," Mom said.

"But he's dead!"

"All those guys are dead."

"But they weren't, they didn't . . . !"

Dad mussed Ray's hair, convinced he was simply being cute. He failed to understand that his only son had been cursed—that he was going to die a violent early death unless he quit the game he adored.

The next day, Ray refused to go to practice for his Fall Ball team. He was sick, he said. A terrible stomachache. Then, when Dad came downstairs that Saturday morning to take him to a double header, Ray, still in his pajamas, refused to budge from the couch.

Dad put down the equipment bag, the bats clunking together like bones. "Be stupid, see if I care," he said before going out to mow the lawn. Mom took a less direct approach, lecturing him that evening about traits that stood out to her when she conducted job interviews. "Hard work," she said. "Dedication." She made her hands into fists when she spoke the word "Tenacity."

There were objections and arguments from teammates and coaches as well, but Ray, afraid to admit the truth and hounded more than most young ball players by the slave driver of superstition (eating seven Gummi Bears before every game, licking the word "hit" into his right palm before every at bat), told everyone he was out for the season. With some, he hinted at a mysteriously enduring illness; in front of others, he prodded a supposedly tender knee. The following spring, he declared himself out of the game for good.

—⁓—

By Anna's request, they went to Parmatown to see *Prelude to a Kiss*, which Ray took as an auspicious omen. He sat next to her in the darkened theater, watching her slim fingers prowl for popcorn. He tried to focus on the film, but when the spirit of the old man climbed into the body of the bride, Ray didn't know what to think except that he wished he was Alec Baldwin because that, he was pretty sure, would have made him the man of this girl's dreams.

At the end of the night, they sat in the Crown Vic in her drive, talking this and that.

"Do you believe in the supernatural?" she asked, eyes closed, head against the rest.

"You mean like God? Heaven?"

"Sort of."

Ray had believed in the efficacy of Gummi Bears, the potent correlation between a hand-licked word and success at the plate. There were long, harrowing days when Ray believed that fate, unimpressed with the huge step he'd taken to avoid it, still had a plan to make him pay.

"I'm a realist at heart," he said, lying through his teeth.

Anna opened her eyes. She tried to make her skirt reach her knees. "I think there's always something more." She went on to talk about expanding one's world. The idea was to move out and out and out and—who knew?—you might eventually run up against then through the wall between this world and another. Movement, travel—it was, she declared, the Viviani way. Once a year, her parents went to spend a month with relatives on the coast of the Adriatic. An older sister taught English in Japan before settling there for good. A brother, instead of going straight to college, was working at a cannery in Alaska. Anna herself had spent two weeks in Paris as a sophomore, and next year, for college, she was determined to go somewhere far away—to Colorado, Arizona, maybe even L.A. Transfixed again by her presence, Ray could do little more than grin and nod and repeat "that's great, that's great!" like a wide-eyed pull string doll. What he said about his own plans he could not recall. There were a few long silences, during which he was too painfully present in the moment for his brain to function. He studied her hand on the seat, palm up, fingers curled like a question mark. When he braved a look into her eyes, his body began to tremble.

The porch light came out of nowhere—jolting him like a bean ball to the head. Anna turned to the glow and began to giggle, as if it were a well-timed joke. "I had so much fun," she said.

"You did?" For the life of him, he could not remember her response, but he was sure it had been beautiful. And filled with sweetness. With the exception of a soft, long kiss on the lips, this had seemed at the time the absolute perfect way to end the perfect evening.

—∞—

Ray looks in the rear view mirror. Eli shifts. His eyes open momentarily, and then, lucky little devil, he's back to his cozy, animal dreams.

"Okay," a new caller says. "Here's one: 2002, first game of the year vs. the Chiefs."

"Sure, sure," Zelonka says. "The one and only Dwayne Dupree Rudd."

Dwayne Rudd—the fool who too soon celebrated a victory by taking off his helmet and chucking it into the air. For his behavior, he earned an unsportsmanlike conduct penalty and, even though the game clock had expired, the Chiefs were granted another play, which they used to kick the game-winning field goal. A shiny new season, a shiny new way to lose. Ray, brand new to Philadelphia then, had been sitting alone in a smoke-choked sports bar nursing a headless Yuengling, peering up at a tiny TV by a bathroom that breathed urine every time the door swung open. He'd been the only one with even the slightest interest in his home team's fate.

"So let me get this straight," Zelonka says. "Rudd shows a little self-control, we win that game, finish 10-6. We're still a half game behind the Steelers."

"Yeah," the caller says. "But then we get the Jets in the playoffs instead. We beat them, remember? In week eight?"

"The Jets? Really?" Zelonka is both surprised and upset about having been brought face-to-face with the limits of his knowledge of local sports history; however, he quickly recovers. "Look, if you want to change something why don't you just have your genie climb into the playoff game, wave his wand, and say, 'Northcutt catches the pass.' The Browns kill the clock, beat the Steelers, and move on to Oakland the following week."

Oakland once again. The Oakland Raiders. Red Right 88. Sipe drops back, bounces, steps forward, lofts that ill-fated ball into the end zone.

"Hey, I'm a Browns fan," the caller says by way of defense. "Aim low is the idea. The meek shall inherit the ring."

"Ha, ha, that's a good one, my friend. You have yourself a Merry Christmas."

Discipline, of course, is the moral of this story. The ability to—in the heat of the moment—do the smart thing, despite strong impulses to the contrary. Ray, having reflected long and hard on the cautionary tale of his mismatched parents, had approached his own choice of partner in a most careful and deliberate way. He dated around for years, refusing on at least three occasions to succumb to the powerful temptations of inertia or really good sex. Finally, he found Dorie through an online dating service. He remembered having devoted a painfully self-conscious evening to creating his profile: wracking his brains for a distinctive screen name; writing a bio with an appropriate degree of intrigue; selecting the right photograph; enumerating likes and dislikes, hobbies and affiliations. The next night, a glutton for punishment, he ran it past Mark and Moose while they sucked down wings at the Winking Lizard.

"Write 'ex-athlete,'" Moose said. "Chicks love that."

"And animals," Mark added.

"Yes, if you're an ex-animal, that's a definite plus."

When all was said and done, Ray began to think of his profile as a baseball card, himself as a journeyman infielder stuck deep in a pack next to the chalky, brittle rectangle of gum. There were better catches, no doubt, but he was a more than serviceable player in the game.

When he proposed to Dorie, he'd been thirty-two—ten years

older than both his parents when they took the plunge. He knew from her profile, from her demeanor during a year's worth of carefully considered dates, that they were compatible in the most important ways: evenly degreed, politically liberal, avid about the performing arts. Over time, he learned that their lovemaking brought mutual satisfaction if not blood-steaming passion. But despite his deliberate game plan, despite the optimal conditions he created, he now finds himself at a loss when he imagines returning to Philadelphia after the holidays, the weight of another pedestrian year bearing down upon him.

Ray brakes hard, realizing at the last moment that the light before him is red. He squeezes the wheel, looks behind at the boy who has not moved. Eli—or someone like him—had been part of the plan, of course. But hadn't he, at some point, become a part of the problem as well? The potty training, the long bouts of inexplicable screaming, the wild animal desires. All the nefarious strategies the little bugger has employed to keep Ray and Dorie exhausted and irritable and forever at home. And if that weren't bad enough, in a few short months, there'd be another one to deal with.

The red light looks down at him—a wide open eye, livid, judgmental. Ray sticks out his tongue, and the signal turns green. He smiles. It's a small victory, but he'll seize whatever win he can.

—◊—

Ray and Anna went out a second time and a third, the dates (a mushroom pizza at Sforzo's, an open skate at Winterhurst) spaced by Anna just far enough apart so as to obscure her motives. For the fourth date, Ray was invited over to the house. Mr. and Mrs. Viviani stayed upstairs, and they watched the end of a Grant and Hepburn movie. Ray, distracted by the narrow space between their bare knees on the sofa, listened as Anna spoke again of future plans with such passion, such intimidating specificity, that all Ray could do was root hard for her, knowing she did not need such support, that every trophy in life would be one day on her shelf.

"Would you mind combing my hair?" she asked, a request so out of the blue that Ray felt he'd won the lottery. Despite the full-tilt central air, his body burned red. Somehow, he recovered, nodded, glanced down as she shifted her bottom on the sofa. With trembling hand, he placed comb on top of head and drew it down, the teeth gentle against her skull, down down the smooth cataract of freshly shampooed hair, stopping an inch above the visible band of her panties before starting the whole tantalizing process once again.

Meanwhile, Anna talked. What came across was her wild popularity, her thorough connectedness to all kinds of people who mattered: those older, adventurous siblings; a handful of nearly daring cousins; several cool and quirky aunts to whom she was especially close; loads of friends—student government friends, national merit semifinalist friends, church friends, volunteer friends. Along the way, she made occasional mention of two boys she'd known since diapers, one with whom she often and at all hours spent serious time.

In the face of such talk, Ray could have slumped into a depression. He could have seethed with jealousy or let loose with rage. But the truth of the matter was this: none of the appealing people she spoke about—not a single one—was just then combing her lovely hair!

After Anna saw him off with yet another breezy "Thanks so much," he sped home, intending to race up to his room and stay on the phone with her until the sweet sun rose again. But when he came through the door, the cloud of a bitter argument between his parents hung oppressively low, bringing down his mood and obliterating his confidence. Instead of calling her, he tossed and turned in bed, kicking himself for awkward lulls in the conversation, a comment Anna probably misconstrued as stupid or inappropriate.

The next morning, Ray woke late, slow and sick with hopelessness. Mark, after failing to cheer him on the phone, appeared minutes later at the front door, dragged him out of the house, into his Chevette, and over to Mezar's, the underground bowling alley just a few tantalizing doors down from the shoe store at which Anna had just given her two week notice.

Ray picked up his ball and stepped onto the approach. The rack rose, and the pins gleamed at him like a set of attractive teeth.

"You've been out with The One four times now and, well, what have you got to show for it?"

Ray took a deep breath and three-stepped it to the foul line, releasing the ball over the second arrow. The lanes were dry, so his ball broke hard—and a smidge too soon—striking the head pin at a bad angle, leaving the seven wobbling on one side and the ten standing firm on the other.

Mark lay down across the row of plastic seats, smiling smugly.

"Look," Ray said. "Let me do things at my own pace."

"If it was me . . ."

"If it was you, she would have slapped you in the face a month ago."

Mark laughed. "Time's running out. The One is leaving for Boulder in a week!"

Ray, trying to block his friend out of his mind, stepped again to the approach, gazed into the void framed by the two remaining pins. Vaguely, he thought of Gummi Bears, a magic word that might be licked into his palm. It was virtually impossible to pick up the 7-10 split, but an extra pin here and there might make a difference in who would win this game.

He let out a deep breath. He bent his knees and then step step stepped again, releasing the ball, knowing well before it happened that it would hook right between the pins.

"And the kick is good!" Mark said, hands raised, mozzarella stick like a cigar in his mouth. "The Browns are Super Bowl champs!"

Ray sat down at the table and scratched his score in the box. So much for the foundation frame.

"Boulder's near Denver, right?" Mark said. "If you're not going to kiss her, have the courage to call this girl what she is: a traitor!"

Ray made the face of a boy after a swallow of spoiled milk. In 1987 and 1988, the Browns—good once again, better than they'd ever been in Ray's still young life—made it to within a game of the Super Bowl. Both times, however, John Elway and the Broncos—the Denver effing Broncos—beat Cleveland in dramatic, terrible ways that have continued to haunt the city. The Drive. The Fumble. Every loss, it seemed, had to have a powerfully pithy name.

"She's got a scholarship," Ray said by way of defense. "And there's more family out there. Cousins or something. She has her reasons."

"I'll never understand you."

"Do me a favor: go up there and throw another gutter ball."

As Mark stepped to the approach, Ray recalled that wonderful Winterhurst date—holding Anna by the waist as she scooted tentatively around the rink, "Life is a Highway" blaring from the speakers above. Afterward, when she stood from the bench where she'd taken off her skates, she cried, "Oh, my ankles," a theatrical frown on her face. "I hope I can make it to the car!"

"Would you like to be carried?" Ray asked.

She looked at him, brows flinching, teeth hidden by bright, thoughtful lips. "Maybe," she said. "We'll have to see."

A thrilling message in code: be patient, she seemed to be saying. Don't force things. You may not carry me now, but someday. Maybe, he thought, the night of their wedding, over the threshold of their brand new home?

The explosion of pins into the pit brought Ray back to the moment. Mark spun around, a fist of victory in front of his face.

Ray looked down at the score sheet. He wanted so badly to beat his friend, but now, if he was going to stand a chance, he'd have to strike out.

—⁂—

"Back in '99," Zelonka bellows, "you know who was still on the board when we drafted Tim Couch? Everybody! Because he was THE FIRST FRICKIN' PICK! We could have had anybody else—anybody at all! McNabb. The Edge. Holt. Champ Bailey! And that's just off the top of my pretty little head!"

Anna, Anna, Anna—she's out in the open now, running rough-shod over Ray's mind, juking, finding all the holes, evading his valiant attempts to knock her ghostly figure out of bounds. He's braking and turning and heading back over the bridge to the city's South Side, to where Anna used to live. A numbered street, an enclosed porch. The rest will come to him—he's certain he can get there by feel. On West 14th, he's distracted by a sign for the Christmas Story house and turns, rolling slowly down the street, savoring the winter-weary homes like the highlights of a game-winning drive. Anna lived nearby, the next street over if memory serves.

In front of the tourist attraction, a bundled-up woman and her three kids stand on the lawn while the father leans against an SUV snapping shots. California plates make him think again of Brian Sipe—the drop back, the bounce, the step forward, the release. Red Right 88.

A few days before Anna left for Colorado, he stood on her front porch, her warm hand in his, and instead of saying "Please don't go" or "I want to be with you," he said, without thinking, "I'm sorry."

"Sorry? For what?"

They'd held hands all the way back from a cozy coffee shop on Kenilworth, and instead of ending the evening with a long-sought-after kiss, he found himself apologizing for taking up so much of her precious time.

Ray makes a few more turns and drives down what he's sure is her street. He's nervous, fidgety, as if he's half his age and going to pick her up for their very first date. Yes, there it is, that one—there's the screened in porch. No, no, didn't her house also have a brick driveway? (He remembered tripping once over a pushed up chunk of red; she laughed, and he, stupidly grinning, wished he'd never been born). Perhaps it had been paved over long ago? He tries to conjure the address, confuses it with twenty years of his own residences and phone numbers and online passwords. The numbers swirl around him, thick and without sequence, while Zelonka goes over Cleveland's top five draft disasters.

As he reaches the end of the street, Ray begins to think her house might have been on the other side of the overpass. He heads back to W. 14th and drives across the interstate bridge, while a caller goes on to criticize Donovan McNabb, the quarterback picked second in the '99 draft.

"I can't believe those Philly fans booed his selection," Zelonka says. "That guy had some wheels. Even with our porous offensive line, Mr. McNabb would have made stuff happen out there. We would have won games!"

"All I remember," the caller says with a chuckle, "is the dude blew chunks during that one Super Bowl."

"Brian, Brian, my friend, do the words SUPER and BOWL mean anything to you?"

"Of course . . ."

"McNabb got there! He reached the frickin' Promised Land!"

On Ray's right appears Lincoln Park. Stopped at the light, convinced he's in the wrong place again, he finds himself watching a group of young guys playing football. A tall fellow in a Patriots jersey backpedals like a pro and lets the ball fly. His receiver is wide open, but the ball slips through the lumbering boy's hands.

When the light turns green, Ray pulls over to the curb and watches another play. He quickly counts the guys. Thirteen. He glances back at Eli, still deep in dreamland.

The next play is a sweep. The pitched ball lands in the running back's gut, and he tucks it in, trying to bowl over a defender, who wraps his arms around a leg until two more teammates arrive to plough him into the turf.

Ray puts a blanket over Eli. He steps from the car, pushes the button on his keychain to lock the doors. Leaning against the hood, blowing into his hands to warm them, he watches a few more incomplete passes and a change of possession that leads to even more ineptness. All of this makes him hungry for competition. He remembers those old, sweet, fate-free days: sprinting onto the baseball diamond, top of the first, rocking back and forth on his feet, chomping gum, plocking his well-seasoned glove with a fist. He remembers stepping into the box, licking that one-word incantation into the palm of his hand. The pure joy of bringing the bat around late in order to slap a fastball past the first baseman who'd drifted too far from the bag. At such moments, anything might happen—a double, a triple. Toss in a wild throw to the cut off man and Ray might very well find himself right back at home, pummeled by teammates for scoring the game-winning run. That hunger did not disappear after Ray had broken up so painfully with his beloved sport. It came out in bowling, in pick up hoops, in holiday football games, where Ray was the unquestioned two-way star. His mother found Ray's participation in football both dangerous and inexplicable. One Thanksgiving afternoon, as he stood on the back porch, pulling off his muddy sweatshirts and pants, she leaned back from the stove and simply said, "You make no sense at all." But Ray was sure his reasoning was irrefutable: by quitting baseball, he'd dodged a fatal bullet. Sure football was more dangerous, but it wouldn't be fair of fate to switch the rules of the game and kill him on a simple run up the middle.

"Room for one more?" he calls out, his voice thin against a sudden gust of wind.

A few guys from the offensive team's huddle turn to study his easy approach. Not guys—boys. They're sixteen, seventeen at the most, and only two or three possess the powerful, precocious bodies that would make Ray second guess his decision to play.

The tall boy in the Patriots jersey—Tom Brady, of course—breaks into an ironic smile. "Sure, man. You're with us."

Another boy—his teammate, a beer-breathing squirt in an oversized Drew Brees shirt—says, "We're the Saviors, by the way. And they're the Dicks."

"Devils!" a long-faced kid from the other side—Peyton Manning— cries.

"Same thing," Brees says.

"To be totally honest," Manning says, hands on his hips. "I don't think teams are fair now."

"What?" Brady turns from the huddle. "You think a pathetic old man's going to be the difference?" He winks at Ray like they've been best buddies for years.

"No, no, you were a guy short anyway. I'm just saying."

"Stop saying and start playing," Brady says. "I don't mind sore losers, but you should really wait to mope until your ass has been officially kicked."

Ray smiles, remembers to glance back at the Prius. It's no more than 100 feet away, parked by the curb. He doesn't see any movement in the backseat. Game on!

For the first series, Brady tells Ray to block, which is all well and good. As an ex-athlete, he understands the need for the new guy to prove himself. On defense, the Devils' quarterback—the pouty Peyton Manning—decides to pick on him. The first play is a slant, and Ray slips on the snow-mushy field when he makes a lunge to knock the pass down. A completion, but a negligible gain. The next play is a button hook—another completion to his man—and while Ray stands hands on hips at the line, he hears a few of his teammates begin to grumble. On the third play, Manning decides to break the bank with a bomb. Despite the field conditions, Ray stays stride for stride with the receiver, and if the ball had not been yards underthrown, he would have hauled the damn thing down.

Ten, fifteen minutes pass in this way—back and forth, neither team breaking through—and Ray, feeling neglected, comes back to the huddle about ready to blow.

"Alright, Jamie you go wide," Brady says. "Ten steps and cut across the middle."

Jamie says, "Jamie does many amazing things, but he does not under any circumstances go over the middle."

Another boy volunteers for the mission, but two others suggest a much, much better idea—a double reverse—which they take turns explaining in giddy detail.

"That's a single reverse," Brady says, rolling his eyes. "You're only changing directions once."

The two boys do the math again; they draw diagrams in the air.

"How bout we run a Megan?" suggests a beefy boy in a Ravens toque. "It's a simple down and in."

A few Saviors chuckle into their sleeves. Brady steps back from the group and barks, "Say one more thing about Megan, and I'll kick your ass."

Ray sees in the boy's hard eyes a whiff of worry; it occurs to him that this Brady, brimming with confidence on the field, is totally in love with the girl in question, but she is probably having little if any of it. It's enough of an opening. "Come on, man," Ray says. "Hit me long. I'll beat my guy, no problem."

The boys turn to Ray as if he's sprouted a second and more hideous old man head.

"Post play."

Brady shrugs, laughs, clearly relieved by the change of subject. "Okay, grandpa," he says. "Don't make me look like a fool."

Over the last several plays, Ray's defender has developed quite the attitude. He's been playing Ray close, bumping him off the line, tossing mild, uninventive trash into his face after every play. Ray steps to the line, blows on his hands. Across from him, the defender's mouth smokes. Before he knows what's happening, Ray finds himself falling in love with this moment: the cold, the wind from out of nowhere, the puffing boy in mud-swiped sweats, the dull ache in his legs, the suck of shoes against wet ground, the dark, leafless trees waving at him from beyond. It is the present, and he is alive inside it, a snug space of time that seems so curiously extended—a drop of water hovering on the tip of an icicle—that he's stunned to hear Brady squash it with a gutteral "Go!" Ray steps towards and then spins around his lunging defender, using three fingers to remain upright, and then he flies, turning after ten long steps, eyes up, hands out for the ball that is spinning through the air. Ray's fast—always has been—but the pass is dropping down too far in front of him. He should pull up, just let it go, but he's close enough if he stretches and he's stretching, the ball on the fingertips of his left hand, it's in his palm, it's back into the air. He brings his right hand out, slips, falls, goes down hard. Pain rips through his arm as he bounces, slides, turns, the wet pigskin trapped against his stomach underneath a vice-like grip.

A catch! A touchdown, damn damn damn it! His teammates whoop it up as Ray, trying to hold onto the thrill, wonders what the hell he's done—the pain still coming, sharp waves and angry laser beams.

Beer breath blows over him. "Grandpa here's got some real wheels."

Ray opens his eyes to see Brees crouching, agog as an archeologist who's brushed to the surface the intact skull of an Ice Age beast. "I'm done, fellas," he says.

"Dumb? Did he just say he's dumb?" the voice is unfamiliar—it could be any of them.

"Done. Finished." He sits up, but he cannot let go of his arm because he is certain it will fall off and the blood will run out of him and he will die.

"Maybe we should get you to the emergency room," a big-eyed boy in an Aaron Rodgers jersey suggests.

"Everybody's a quarterback," Ray thinks, "but not one of them's a Brown."

"Hey, if you guys leave," Manning whines, "I want you to know it's a forfeit."

"It's halftime, pud," Brady says, clapping him on the shoulder.

Ray stands, and several boys surround him, subdued and weirdly solicitous. The sympathy is a salve upon his injured heart.

"I'll just drop him off," Brady says. "Lutheran's right around the corner."

"No, no. I'm good."

"Come on. My luck you'll drop dead, and I'll have that on my conscience for the rest of my life."

Ray smiles, grimaces, gingerly maneuvers his body onto the passenger seat. Before he closes the door, he notices in front of him the back end of a distinctly familiar vehicle. "Eli," he says, voice barely above a mumble.

Manning, hands on hip by the curb, says, "Eli sucks rocks."

Brees playfully grabs him by the neck of his jersey. "How can you say that, man? About your own damn brother!"

There's a smattering of laughter until Brady parts them with a hand. "Back in ten," he says, sliding into the driver's seat.

"I have a boy," Ray says. "Eli."

Brady slaps his leg. "Congratulations, man."

"He's in my car. That one, right there." Ray closes his eyes, and on the inside of his lids is an image of himself alone on a wide field, fans jeering while he slouches toward the bench to watch in futility the last sad moments of a championship game.

—⁓—

Back in his own car, Eli snug behind him, Ray slowly moves his right arm across his body. A sharp pain continues to bullet back and forth between shoulder to elbow, but it no longer makes him want to wretch. Nothing, he's almost sure, has been broken.

He starts the engine, and pulls away without so much as a wave. There's nowhere else to go now but back to his old home—the place where he learned so well the lessons of pain and loss. December, 1980, he thinks. Seven years old and never had life been so full of joy. Christmas shopping, ordinarily a deathly bore, was brightened by the Halloween-like colors of brown and orange. Sears, J. C. Penney, Stop-N-Shop—department stores and grocery stores had all come down with Browns Fever. Mom, neither knowing nor caring much about what was at stake, made a pan of muffins, let Ray and Mark spoon brilliant orange batter into paper baking cups.

The Friday before Christmas, his father took him to an auto parts store, where he waited in line for over an hour so Mike Pruitt and Clay Matthews could sign a balloon that wound up popped and in the garbage by the end of the day. No matter—he'd had the opportunity to shake the players' hands and wish them both good luck. After the team clinched the division title, Ray bought the "Twelve Days of a Cleveland Browns Christmas," rushed home, snapped the plastic chip in the hole of the 45, and played the song again and again. Like the singers of the song, he craved nothing more than "a Rutigliano Super Bowl team."

Again, he recalls the last minute of that fateful playoff game, the

Browns driving toward the open end of the stadium, the wind livid off the lake. They made it all the way to the Raiders fourteen-yard line. On the radio, Gib Shanley said, "Buckle your seatbelts," as he did for all the nailbiters through the course of the season. Uncle Ben, who'd earlier let Ray belt him to the couch with a wound up bedsheet, had long since broken loose to pace the room, beer in hand. Sipe took the ball from DeLeone, and Ray's father stood, hands to unshaven cheeks and then rising slowly past ears into hair, the fingers growing out from either side of his head like feelers or horns. After the interception, he remained in that position, as if the worst were still to come. Uncle Ben slammed his beer on a tray table and dropped a trail of curse words right out the door, with Mom shouting after him, "It's only a game. You're grown men!" All Ray could remember about that night was the sound of his own snotty tears. Surely, someone must have spoken. Surely, he must have asked for the salt at dinner. Surely, his father must have at some point come into the room to say, "You can't win 'em all."

Ray's life had gone on and on and on, a tight spiral through the air, until it suddenly began to loosen, dying in the hard wind that rushed against it.

"What you gotta do," a new caller says, "is stop talking about the Browns."

"Yeah, yeah. Give me your do-over." Zelonka is already fed up with this troll—that's clear.

"Let them move out of town again. Who the hell cares?"

"No," Zelonka says. "I don't understand what you're saying. It's French or something. No, no—Latin. It's a dead language."

"Zel, you like to tell everyone to face facts, but it's you who has to put down the Crooked River Kool-Aid."

"Thanks Scrooge, but the good people of Northeast Ohio deserve more than your doom and gloom. Eric, you're on the Zelonka Show."

The Kool-Aid, the Kool-Aid, spiked with the rosy viscous goo of romance. Ray realizes that this had been his beverage of choice up until the very end, when he went out with Anna the afternoon before she left for Colorado. They sat opposite of each other on hard plastic chairs in a frigid fast food restaurant, where Anna spent more time smoothing down gooseflesh on her arms than explaining just how terrible it was going to be to leave him behind.

An hour later in her drive, she reached over to crush him close. He looked out the window at a holly bush, feeling without pleasure her breasts flatten against his chest. With hand on her back, he thumbed up and down her vertebrae, read like a blind man the first several chapters of her beautiful bones.

"Well, I gotta go," he'd said, pulling back quickly, wanting to see registered in her eyes the punishment he was trying to inflict.

She smiled—more a curved purse of lips—and said, "I'll miss you." Even now he gives her, wherever she is, the credit of mostly meaning it.

He had loved this person deeply—followed her with a passion— and then it all was over, except for a single letter she floated back to his side of the country in mid-September, which sketched out for him a heart-stopping world she'd quickly made her home. There was a single picture as well, a poorly developed photo from a party at Moose's. He and Anna are sitting close on a picnic bench, stringed lights in a crabapple tree behind them. She's in heels and white capris, wine cooler on a knee, a noncommittal expression on her face. Ray's mouth is open in surprise, his forehead shiny with sweat. For a long time, he'd kept the photograph in his wallet. Where in the world is it now?

Another caller—Susan from Independence: "Losing is what it's all about. Much, much more interesting."

Zelonka snorts. "That's perverse!"

Susan politely disagrees. As a high school English teacher, she's had great success using the Browns to get students to appreciate the unparalleled beauty of Shakespeare's tragedies. In fact, she once presented on this topic at an academic conference.

"Well, well," Zelonka laughs. "This is why I never liked literature. Everybody always dies in the end."

The next caller—Don from University Heights—is back to Red Right 88. His argument is that Sipe should have been benched.

"For McDonald? A rookie? You think Californians are interchangeable or something?"

"He'd already thrown two picks."

"Sipe was the MVP of the NFL! Does that mean anything to you?"

"Conditions were terrible. Why didn't we just keep the ball on the ground?"

"I'll let you in on a little secret," Zelonka says. "Conditions are never perfect. Too much snow, too much wind, small change raining down from the stands upon your head. Sprained thumb, bruised ribs, sore hammy. Bad gas, for crying out loud. What I'm saying is this: the clock starts, you do your best to make things happen. You do what you do, regardless."

Here Ray is, pushing forty, and as his old buddy Mark always reminds him during his biannual trips back home, he has everything most people long for in life—a smart, attractive partner, an adorable child, a comfortable home, a decent job, a modest stash of disposable income—but all he's thinking of now is that damn picture, the one piece of visual evidence that there'd once been another (and much better) life in the making. He's struck by the idea that everything after Anna has been achieved on some secondary plane of existence, a kind of minor league world that, although better than most, has not been the best of the best. It's stupid (of course) to dismiss the second quarter of his life in such a way (and stupider to take for granted the precise length of his own "game" on Earth), but he can't help himself.

"You know," Zelonka continues, "They were called the Kardiac Kids for a reason. When you try a Red Right 88, there's always a chance of Kardiac Arrest. It's the price of doing business, my friends. Price of doing business."

"Zel," Don says. "You are the man, but you're also a little bit off your rocker."

Zelonka laughs. "Look, I had the privilege of chatting with Mr. Sipe at a Browns reunion a few years back. Guess how many days it took that fine gentleman to get over that pass? Any ideas? Hmmm? How about three. That's right, THREE. He's been over it now for as long as some of you listeners have been alive! Oh, I hear some of you out there saying, 'Zel, he cared that little for the most important game of his life?' and I say to you, calm down, take a stiff drink, sample your favorite sedative. The truth is this: he brought great, unforgettable moments to this town. Not the greatest of things, but if you're a real Cleveland fan—a real fan of the game—he gave you one whole glorious thrill ride of a season to remember. That's a real accomplishment. That's a memory this kid in fat man's clothing will take with him to his grave. C.G.—you, my friend, are up on the other side."

Stopped for red, Ray takes the opportunity to move arm across chest a few more times. There is a low current throb, but he's likely going to be fine. When the light changes, he turns onto his parents' street, his head filling with anxious questions: Is the pork loin done?

Overdone? Is Dorie missing breadcrumbs for her side dish master-piece? Will his father—?

A sudden boom. Ray's hand slips from the wheel, and his head jounces like a baby. "Jesus!" he says, looking in the rearview mirror for the hole he's just driven through. Flat tire, alignment, he thinks. Money he doesn't have. He glances over his shoulder, and, sure enough, Eli is shifting back and forth, eyes adjusting to the world.

"Hey, bud. Welcome back."

"Icksmas." The boy points out the window at an inflatable Santa sagging into a browned-out lawn.

"Sleep well?"

"Dare are gifs at home."

"That's right," Ray says, tightening his grip on the wheel, the house a fastball coming at him. "Dinner first, and then all kinds of gifts."

A Night at The Orr House

"I'm sorry," I said, hand to mouth, raising my voice against the jukebox din. "Did you say, 'whore house'?"

Mirabella, the woman to whom I was speaking, moved winter-split lips within inches of mine. "*Orr* House," she said. "As in, Benjamin Orr."

"The musician?" Years before—a bookshelf of selves ago—I'd been faintly acquainted with the world of popular music. "The . . . He was in The Cars?"

She smiled, leaning toward the bar for a long drink of gin.

It occurred to me that I should feel sorry for Mirabella D'Amico, this tipsy slip of a woman I'd not seen since high school, when she'd flirted with invisibility, her frame shapeless beneath the voluminous concert t-shirts she wore every single day. Soon after she transferred to our school, Rick Krieger—my closest approximation of a friend—sought her out at her locker to say, "Ni hao, China Girl, you my favowite Wock and Woller!" From her knees, she looked up, smile thin as a string. Inspired, having the time of his life, Rick belted out a few lines from "Everybody Wang Chung Tonight!"—an insidious earworm that had been inching up the charts. As usual, a step or two behind, I drew textbooks to my chest, cast eyes to the floor, and kept right on going.

"Local rock star deserves a house," Mirabella said. "Don't you think?"

I nodded. In the awkward pause that followed, the pap from the overhead speakers swirled together with the melodies of dimly remembered performers: Blondie, The Clash, Bowie, Madness. The Cars. In my state—at my age—one had become much like the other.

"You want to go see it?"

"The Orr House? Is it open to the public?" I finished my wine. Behind the register, the pincers of the bar clock were coming together at the two. "At this time of night?"

"I'm the curator—it's open whenever I say."

"I don't know. I'm . . . It's been a long . . . Is it—?"

"Right around the corner."

Fifteen minutes earlier, I'd been enjoying a final drink alone when Mirabella lurched against the bar, my name like a charm upon her lips. Although disturbed by the assault, I managed to blurt hers out in return. Pleased—overjoyed—she slid onto the stool beside me to calculate the number of years since we'd seen each other last. Now, with this surprising invitation, I suspected she might be looking for something more than just another patron for her strange museum. Vaguely, I was flattered. On the street, she might have been called attractive more often than not. However, I'd known for years that I was not the kind of man to leave a bar with a woman, regardless of her allure. I escaped to the bathroom to figure a plan. When I returned, excuses upon my lips—grieving a sudden loss, needing rest for an early flight out—Mirabella stood before me in a pert leather jacket, hands out for mine, eyes like a pop song that refused to release the brain.

"I have to settle—"

"You're all paid for."

"No, no." I reached for my wallet. "I can't accept—"

"It's on me." She dismissed my bills with a fling of fingers and weaved toward the door.

What I craved was quiet—the pristine anonymity of a well-appointed hotel room; however, I saw I had no choice but to do as she desired. A half hour, a few encouraging assessments—that, I vowed, would be the extent of my service for the night.

To my surprise, The Orr House was no kitschy ruse, but a sincere labor of love: there were album covers and signed concert posters; a sprawling collage of ticket stubs from Boston to Los Angeles; glossy, blown-up shots of the dimple-chinned heartthrob in every tilt and mood. I paced the room, appreciating artifacts, all the while thinking that Mirabella, although quite unusual in her obsession, was not unlike most natives of this hapless city of my birth. To counter the negativity—the burning river, the racial tension, the corrupt politics, the chronic failures of sports teams— Clevelanders clung to their few well-known stars. Anyone who'd spent formative years here was claimed: Paul Newman, Langston Hughes, Bob Hope. There was that actress too—the African American, the one who never appeared to age. As Mirabella spoke about recent acquisitions—Mr. Orr's diamond studded earring, his department store credit card—I noticed all the tell-tale signs of the typical Cleveland booster: the nervous eyes, the apologetic tone, the quickening of speech in direct proportion to the assumed indifference of her audience. For the second time this evening, I thought I should pity her.

"Why don't we take a break," Mirabella said, waving me into a checkerboard tiled room cramped with a vending machine, a pair of plastic tables, and a handful of folding chairs. This, I was informed, was Panorama, the Orr House's "spectacular" snack bar. She opened a cabinet above the sink and brought down a fresh bottle of bourbon. "Nightcap?" she asked, snapping the seal.

I nodded. One quick drink. What had it ever cost me to be generous in this regard?

"I've probably had enough," Mirabella said, although this did not stop her from pouring a stiff one for herself.

"So did Mr. Orr really live here? Is this where he came of age?"

She handed me a glass. "Did Ralphie live in the Christmas Story house?"

I nodded, vaguely aware of the reference. The strong ones, the fortunate ones, I supposed, never had to worry about what actually happened in a given place. Selective memories, careful purchases, a healthy imagination—these were quite enough to make any house other than what it was.

Drinks in hand, we went down glow-in-the-dark stairs into the basement. In front of us, a long black-draped case rested upon a ping pong table.

"It's not what it looks like," she said.

I did not doubt her. However, that did not prevent me from remembering this morning: the frigid chasm of the church, the sparsely peopled pews, the brittle priest swinging a censer over the casket. Through the cloud of smoke, I spied Father twitching in his wheelchair. "Mine," he seemed to mumble. Or was it "Crime"? I turned away and raced the zipper of my coat up to the chin.

Mirabella counted to three and whipped away the dark cloth with a magician's flourish, revealing a glass case inside of which sparkled the body of a well-preserved guitar.

"Stingray," I said, after moments of silent appreciation.

"Are you a musician?"

"Me? Hardly. I just read the plaque."

Mirabella smiled into her drink.

"Was this one of his?"

"Of course." She tapped the glass with a broken nail. "See the signature?"

"A pretty penny, I imagine."

"Gobs. But when do you not pay through the nose for what you really really want?"

Embarrassed, I shifted attention to the faintly familiar song that had begun to fill the room. It was a brooding melody, punctuated by strange laser beams of sound. Then came Mr. Orr's voice—the cold, spare, staccato lines I'd not heard in years. In an instant, I was my seventh grade self on Rick Krieger's unmade bed, a Cars album dangling before my eyes. On the cover was a startling figure: a redhead in a dark yet see-through suit, her eyes closed, arm flung across brow, body stretched across the sloping hood of a sports car. I'd been drawn first to the woman's belly button, but after a few stunned moments dared to look further down, between scissoring legs, at what first appeared to be only an errant line of the sketch.

"Hard yet?" Rick asked, the record dropping onto the turntable like a fist into palm. "It's a fucking cartoon, but one look and I'm stiff as a board."

The vinyl spun. The needle drew the bouncy sounds of the first track into the air.

"Hear that?" He tipped back on his chair to punch me in the thigh. "Like bedsprings? It's the wang wang wang of people doing the nasty!"

I nodded, as if this were common knowledge. Even then—young as I was—I knew Rick was bullying me into a world that would demand more than I'd ever be able to give.

Later, at his front door, he stacked albums in my hands. "You don't know this one? Here. Mary and Joseph, are you a homo? A Russian spy? Here," he said, shoving another at my face. "And this one—all the way."

"Shall we continue?" Mirabella said.

I nodded, following her to a doorway over which a glittery banner cheered: "HEY LET'S GO WITH THE UPBEAT SHOW!"

"This place is my favorite," she said with a sigh. "The innocent early years."

By the entrance of the dim, walk-in closet of a room, Mirabella pushed a button and a surf-inspired number splashed through the speakers. I moved toward the centerpiece—a blown up black and white photograph of a group of sharply dressed musicians. These, the plate below informed me, were The Grasshoppers, the house band for an early version of The Upbeat Show, the local program I never knew existed. Immediately, my attention was drawn to the right side of the frame, where a striking young man stood in suit and tie, mouth open before the mic, immaculate white guitar high against his body, a suave comma of hair above the eyes. Benjamin Orzechowski.

"His nickname was Benny Eleven Letters."

I nodded. I could appreciate the fact of words that simply could not be pronounced.

"A lot of big acts appeared on this show," Mirabella said, hand guiding my eyes toward photographs of a variety of other performers. "You see The Who there. And Stevie Wonder. The Rolling Stones . . ."

I studied all of these fresh-faced boys. I admired their energy, their fire, their uncanny ability to seduce an audience. What had each endured in order to make it to this stage? What secret burdens had they carried with them into their even more famous future lives?

"You know, The Cars really should be in the Rock Hall. Cheap Trick is, for God's sake. And Joan Jett."

"Maybe someday soon."

"It would definitely mean more visitors."

"Is business poor?"

"The Orr House could always use more customers," she said, her wink less flirtatious than fatigued.

Nervous, exhausted myself, I looked for a place to put down my glass. "I really should call a cab."

"No," she said. "Please."

Before I could say another word, I was being moved through a door into another close, dark space—this time a miniature theater with two chairs facing a bright square moon of a screen. In the near-dark, I was transported to spring of senior year, when Rick decided it was high time that my eighteen-year-old self enjoy the proximity of a girl or two. "You ready at last to be a man?" he asked, clapping me on the back. I nodded, and he made all the arrangements; for him, it was a real public service. What followed for me were long, damp-armed nights of anxiety—Father's front door leer, the dreadful drive to the girl's house, the crippled conversations, the humiliating isolation of bucket seats. In between journey and return, there were the awkward hours in dark theaters, where I had neither courage nor much desire to try for a hand or knee. Years later, during the brief, plodding courtship of my wife, there'd been dates in other dark spaces. From the beginning, she—unlike the others—has been charmed by my diffidence, by my exemplary reserve. "You're the perfect gentleman," became her ecstatic refrain. It was a sentiment with which her parents heartily agreed.

Those days of "perfection," however, had been gathering dust for years on my shelf of selves. For better or worse, there was only right now—this small space, this relative stranger, the flicker and flash not of a romantic comedy but of a low-key interview with the members of The Cars years after the group had disbanded. The leader, the long, gaunt songwriter whose name I failed to recall, was doing most of the talking. He wore dark sunglasses and periodically wiggled a finger in his ear. When he said he liked to hide inside his lyrics, I thought with great sadness about how all kinds of words—either by accident or intention—could elude even one's most fervent attempts to unpack them.

Eventually, the camera panned to Mr. Orr, who sported yellow-tinted sunglasses and a Cleveland Browns jersey that looked three sizes too large for him.

Mirabella said, "This, of course, was when he was dying."

I nodded, even though the musician's death was news to me.

"How about I put on something else?"

"No, that's okay."

"Well, I really think it's . . . spoiling the mood."

What mood? I wondered. I had not known there'd been a mood in the way she seemed to be suggesting. I glanced in her direction and saw that her eyes had very little of the bedroom about them, unless that bedroom part meant covers and an eye mask and eight hours of undisturbed rest.

"You remember *Fast Times*—the movie?" she asked. "Phoebe Cates climbing out of the pool in that red bikini?"

I crossed my legs. "I was not that kind of boy."

"Sure you weren't."

"Please believe me."

"Come on. Remember the song in that scene?"

"I'm going to assume it was The Cars."

"'Moving in Stereo.' You want me to cue it up?"

"No, no. I believe I'm good."

A few moments later, Mirabella slapped her lap and stood, moving behind a dark, poorly hung curtain. Left alone, I studied the doomed man in the Browns shirt until I drifted back to the evening before, sitting far from so-called family and friends at the funeral home, arms crossed before a slick slide show my aunts had lovingly created. There were Mother and Father, Brian and me. Over and over, in all manner of poses and combinations. Interspersed throughout were several photographs of me alone throughout the years, grinning with whatever teeth I had beside a birthday cake, on a banana bike, before a tinsel-laden Christmas tree. Taken together, the show told a cozy, wordless tale of familial love that brought nearly everyone to tears. Afterwards, I was accosted by aunts and uncles and cousins, all of whom said that we'd been such good, good boys.

And they were right. Brian and I were good—respectful to elders, uncommonly unspoiled, grateful for all we'd been given, like, for example, the crisp new dollar bills Father would pin beneath the hooves of our identical piggy banks sometime while we slept. One night—I believe I was six—my brother whispered through the bamboo screen between our beds: "You do more, you get more."

I glanced at the curtain and saw Mirabella's body moving behind it. At any moment, I expected Mr. Orr and his bandmates to be replaced by the beautiful young girl rising from the pool to the ponderous, ethereal beat of the song that had been seeping back into my brain. Instead, there was another sound—a familiar thrum, a domestic roll and ping. It was three o'clock in the morning, and Mirabella was drying her clothes. For a third time, I thought I should pity her.

When she reappeared, I cleared my throat. I swallowed. "Did I ever call you names?"

She raised her brows.

"You must remember. China Girl? Wock and Woller?"

"I was Vietnamese," Mirabella laughed. "Still am as a matter of fact."

"A few years after graduation, I finally figured that out."

"My mom told me I'd been on the first copter out of Saigon—you know, the one that went down and killed all those babies. Her tuck-in pep talks were all these variants of, 'You're a survivor!!' Of course the years didn't add up . . ."

"Maybe—"

"I know, I know. To her credit, maybe she just wanted to make me special. Unique beyond all doubt. Well, the thing is, I already was special—beyond my wildest nightmares! The ugly Asian with the outlandishly Italian name. I tell you, it was a long childhood, a long adolescence, of one stupid double take after the other. Years of ching chong, bing bang bongs. Then we moved here, and even though I was a senior with acne and brown skin and strange, slanty eyes, I thought, okay, this is the 'big city' now, more or less. Maybe it's not the end of the world. Maybe I've got a second chance. A clean slate. A new self. I could fit in if only I had a plan."

"And the plan was . . .?"

"Pop music. Dive deep into the local stuff. Declare my love for Benjamin Orr, the blue-eyed hometown star. I was a freak, but music is the universal language . . . or so I thought." She touched lips to her drink. "Well, you saw how that worked out. Or you would have, had you ever dared to look up from your books."

"I do apologize."

Mirabella shrugged. "Anyway, I was too late . . . for The Cars, I mean. By the time I became their number one fan, they just weren't so popular anymore. People were moving on."

Over the ping and hum of the dryer, Mr. Orr spoke again, summing up his thoughts about his rock and roll life. "It's been great fun," he said, his voice soft and full of sadness. He expressed a deep pride in being a part of the group. He called his bandmates, "Great people." Then he swallowed hard, raised his brows, and added "About it"—his simple, inelegant goodbye to the world.

"You know," Mirabella said after a time, "I really don't remember you being so damn stiff."

I became short of breath. My underarms prickled.

"And dour. You're like some actor from PBS. I mean, I could totally see you standing in the doorway of an overstuffed drawing room and fingering the brim of a hat in your hands."

The dying man vanished from the screen.

"Well . . . the truth is I am in mourning."

"Oh, I'm—"

"It's the reason I've returned."

"I'm so sorry." She squeezed her hands between her knees. "You want to talk about it?"

I was sorely tempted. From far away, never-uttered words began to gather, finding the ones next to which they knew they belonged.

However, before I could open my mouth, the image of the closed coffin hurtled through, scattering the words in all directions. Behind came Mother, unsteady between her sisters, eyes melting out of sockets, and Father, alone in his wheelchair, mouth like the stretched neck of a shirt, right hand a gnarled scoop against his chest. A week before he died, Brian had called me from his trailer by the lake to tell me that he'd "done the math" and concluded that life was "ninety-seven percent not worth living." In recent years—even when he remembered to take his medication—Brian had made many grim speeches to that effect. Always, and with great verve, I refused to acknowledge his melodramatic view of the world. That night, however, when he went on to say that "someone needs to make a statement," I lost my temper. Perhaps misunderstanding his intent, I told him to be quiet. I told him not to breathe a word.

"Oh, I can't bear this anymore," Mirabella said, standing up to turn off the interview.

Immediately, the room went black. Moments later, I heard the light thump of stockinged feet. There was soft breath, a haunting creak mere inches from my crossed legs. My hands wrung the arms of the chair.

"I've got another idea," she said.

I fully expected the worst. Instead, there was only another curious sound: the twang and plod of a bass guitar between deep, suicidal chasms of silence. Then, from the void, came the lonely voice of Mr. Orr.

"This is 'All Mixed Up.' You know it? All the other recording tracks have been removed."

Stripped of instrumentation, the dead man's voice had a purity I'd never known. By the second verse, my shelf of selves, disturbed without pause during this grim trip home, began at last to tilt. I closed my eyes against the inevitable slide and crash.

When Mirabella's soft hand squeezed mine, I thought I wanted to die. "What are you after?" I asked.

"Ha! What was I before?"

Between stretches of silence, the singer's voice returned to remind the world that he was all mixed up.

"What must I do?'"

There was a sniff—a hint of tears. "It's okay: Stay or go," she said. "The customer's always right."

At that moment, the dryer sounded. My hand was released, but it proved too late. All of those former selves slid down the length of that shelf, dropping one after the other onto the dark, hard floor of my heart. As Mr. Orr laid bare his soul again, I wondered how many of them I'd have to sift through to find the one with a clue about how to be touched.

The Whole Head is Sick
and the Whole Heart is Faint

Father

BEHIND A STAND of browning maples, Erie is a gray and prostrate sky. Hamblin holds the gear shift for a minute before slipping the vehicle into park. Alone on this damp, fog-heavy morning, he recalls a verse from Isaiah: "Fear not, for I am with you; be not dismayed, for I am your God; I will strengthen you, I will help you, I will uphold you with my righteous right hand." It's a passage to which he's often pointed parishioners struggling to cope—with failure in love or occupation, with the loss of long-time spouses, with the flight of grown up children in this peripatetic time.

"Prophets are all well and good," Mrs. Ashley—Nora—told him last week when he stopped by for tea, "but what I could use right about now is a cigarette." She'd just had her hair done—grim, tenacious curls that, he was sad to admit, did little more than highlight her decrepitude. As she spoke, he tried to avoid staring at the tube feeding into her nostrils and the silver tank of oxygen at her feet. It's not that Hamblin hadn't seen his share of bodies breaking down, but he'd always been fond of this Nora—the no-nonsense talk, the blatant flirtations even as her now-dead husband crossed his feet on the recliner nearby. Over the years—less so since her vision had taken such a turn for the worse—he'd enjoyed her bracing dinners. Such good, hearty fare: dense, flavorful meatloaf, chunky chicken potpies, rich casseroles served with warm homemade bread. Afterward, there was always that roomy wing chair to sink into with a delicious spot of tawny port as Nora, once her husband yawned his way to bed, told with great longing eyes the stories about her "singular single days."

Hamblin turns up the heat a notch and gives the car some gas so it won't stall. When he was a boy, he took weekly trips with his parents and siblings to this very beach. Always, he recalls, there was brilliant sun, the opaque water, delightful hours spent molding intricate sand cities, simple lunches of canned fish and bland, processed bread— whatever they could afford. Once upon a time there was Canada, which he imagined as a pristine other world just beyond the horizon; now, though, there's just steel wave upon wave, each more frigid than the one before.

"Wash yourselves," Hamblin thinks, revving the engine again, "Make yourselves clean; Remove the evil of your deeds from My sight." Today, he's got Isaiah on the brain; as Justin, one of his favorite altar boys might say, "the dude's sick with it."

Hamblin glances out the side window. He turns quickly, notices behind him an empty pickup tucked between bold white lines. Still, not a soul in sight. This should not depress him so much. After all, as a parish priest for the last thirty-five years, he's become if nothing else a great connoisseur of human loneliness. The problem is, he loves people—always has—with a passion that has only become more aching over time. There's nothing—not the Bible, not even the miracle of the Eucharist—that he loves more about his vocation than greeting parish- ioners in the crisp morning air after nine o'clock mass. It's the time he's at his best—broadly smiling, shaking hands, offering a witty word for a young man sporting a new beard, taking a child's stuffed toy in hand to perform a brief impromptu drama which she cannot get enough of.

Afterward, back in the rectory for the break between masses, Hamblin is always restless, unnerved by the deathly quiet. Mrs. Ramirez is not there to laugh at his dumb puns between fielding phone calls. Fr. Bonner, the young, damp-faced priest, the earnest ABD, is not there as he is three days a week to, among other things, reinvigorate Hamblin's faith. What he craves more after that first mass of the day is not communion with God, not another cup of coffee, but noise: the thrilling thunder of the organ, the strong, resonant voices of well-practiced lectors, the sudden, delicious screams of babies that make even the hardest parishioners crack into smiles.

A youngish man in a sweatshirt and snug black running shorts appears by the trees clustered at the head of a trail. Surprised, embarrassed, Hamblin busies himself with the radio dial until he gathers the courage to look again. The man is perhaps twenty-five feet away, sitting on the grass, knees out like hairy wings, the soles of shoes pressed hard together for a kiss. He stretches for several more minutes before disappearing into a path that cuts between the trees and dips down closer to the lake.

"Grant me chastity and continence, but not yet," Hamblin thinks, appreciating again St. Augustine's cunning wisdom. He has to hand it to the great church father—the man certainly knew how to divide his one and only life. Maybe, just maybe, if Hamblin had set aside even a few young years for carnal pleasures, he'd not be here now in this particular part of the park.

Hamblin gives the car some gas again and looks toward the trailhead, sending out a short, terrible prayer for the jogger's return.

God, he knows full well, is giving him time to reconsider. Get out, He's crying at the top of his lungs. Go home, make a bowl of maple oatmeal, prop your feet up in front of the morning news. Say mass. Tend to your flock. Prepare for tonight's meeting with the peace committee, where good-hearted men and women will put heads together to work out the details of a new program to help the neighborhood poor. Get sound sleep for a busy tomorrow: there's eight a.m. mass and then he has to bring his stalling vehicle into the shop and have Randy, his long-time mechanic, drive him back to the church so he can get ready for a funeral, a young man, Alan, who slipped from a cliff on a trip with a buddy into the Alaskan wild; in the afternoon, a quick lunch (if there's time) before a cab trip to the Clinic for anointing of the sick; in the evening, pre-Cana with a couple whom, for a host of reasons, he is trying to discourage from the sacrament of marriage.

Hamblin has a busy life, full of responsibility. So many people have come to depend upon him, and he understands that—he really does. But at the same time, he's come to crave something more. For once—for once after all these hard, lonely years—he wants to be a fully human body with another. For once, just once, before his whole sad house of flesh and bones sinks to the earth for good. Why, in God's name, is that so much to ask?

Sometime later, the man in the snug shorts appears at the head of the path again, cooling down on a still lush patch of grass. When he walks by the car, he glances at Hamblin, face flushed from exertion.

Hamblin cannot help himself: he rolls down the window and says, "Gorgeous weather," his voice teetering on an edge.

The man stops, places hands on hips. "November 3rd," he says between well-controlled breaths. "It's a real blessing."

Hamblin smiles. His car has stalled, but it hardly matters. He reaches down to ease the tongue of his belt through the buckle. His head fills with sin, shame, judgment, the resurrection of the body at the end of time. There are times when he's been tempted to speak with stern love into the sweet faces of all those parish widows: "When you die, you are not going to see your husband as he was when alive. You will not be able to touch him or to hear him or to smell him. You will not sit down in cozy chairs and reminisce between sips of sweet drinks about all the wonderful times you enjoyed on good old Earth. When you die, you will not be a body. You will not have eyes or ears, hands or heart. That's what life on Earth was for." At some level, his elderly parishioners must know this terrible fact. If not all of them, at least his Nora, who, with all her ailments, probably can't wait to be released from the flesh.

"What are you up to?" he asks the runner, who continues to stand a few feet away, as if waiting for Hamblin to turn him on.

"Do you have any ideas?"

Hamblin eases open his car door, tries to pour into his face all of the post-service charm he can muster.

The man looks him up and down. He bites his lower lip, and the teeth slide provocatively back into his mouth.

"I have fifty dollars here." Hamblin holds out the bill, a flaccid oblong wafer.

"I see." The man shoots a quick look behind him, as if he's being pursued. "And what exactly would you like me to do?"

Hamblin takes a deep breath—he's arrived beyond shame at the moment of truth. "Anything you can."

The other man smiles—sadly now—before reaching into a pocket to show the priest a badge. "How about I give you a ride to the station?"

Hamblin looks with great longing at the man's flushed but solemn face. His right hand drops between his legs and when he closes his eyes, it becomes—like bread to body—the cool, soft flesh of a long-sought lover. Soon—a year from now, or two or five—Hamblin's body will be a pyramid of bones and dust, but wherever this act causes the other part of him to land, he refuses to believe it won't be a heaven.

Mother

Tonight—and more and more as the days churn by—Nora misses her Edward nearly as much as she misses her beloved cigarettes. She shuffles to the credenza, oxygen a torpedo on wheels behind her. She opens the drawer, lowers her head to the unopened package of Newports that, despite her poor vision, shines like a fresh deck of cards.

Nora would give anything now to have Edward in his recliner, his favorite nature show roaring to life on the TV. She's ashamed to think that she never loved him that much—at least in the messy, sticky way that bodies are driven to be; nevertheless, she bided her time, obliged him in bed, full more often than not with the faith that one day his passion would fall away like a layer of skin, revealing a pink new self that would be content to lie next to (instead of on top of) her with a love pure beyond all measure. From that moment on, whatever time they had left would be a heaven on earth.

But then, one pleasant spring morning, just as glimpses of that new self had begun to emerge, Edward went into the hospital for a lingering cough. A week later, he was dead of pneumonia.

"He is safe at home with the Lord," Fr. Hamblin said, squeezing Nora's shoulder at the cemetery. Jesus, she thought—a Christian's sweet companion, the bastard thief in the night. In the weeks follow-ing Edward's death, Nora's thinking about her savior shot frantically back and forth, like hands in a lake desperate for rescue. The next time her priest came to visit, she with great effort kept the sacrilege to herself.

She presses her talking wrist watch: "The time is 9:55 PM," it says in its grim, indifferent way. If she called Fr. Hamblin right now, she's sure he'd say it was not too late for him to drop by. Lonely himself, he'd be over in minutes to bestow upon her the gift of his warm, human voice.

Nora feels around for the plastic tab on the cigarettes and peels open the box, bringing it to her nose to breath in the tar. At such close range, she can make out the flat, blank heads packed together in rows. It takes her a while, but she's able to nudge one out and place it on her lips. The thrill of eighteen returns: sliding into a booth in Bearden's, a slick haired boy across from her, "All of Me" on the juke-box, the pure white smoke rising from her painted lips in a sensuous twist. The good old days—the hot dream of sex before the shame of during and after.

God knows where the matches are now, but the stove is steps away. Turn on the burner and lean in for a light, wait for spark to find gas, the marriage of which would obliterate the body that's turned like a sick dog against her. The fast track to heaven, if the sky is where it is. More and more frequently, the thought of such an act is what passes for her prayers.

The phone rings, and the cigarette drops from her lips into the fuzzy void below. Maybe, Nora thinks as she feels herself to the kitchen wall, maybe it's Fr. Hamblin calling, miraculously aware of her desire to hear another human voice.

"Hello, hello," Nora says, trying not to sound desperate.

"Oh, Mother," says the voice, a handsome swirl of dread and joy. "Have you heard the news?"

It's Luke—her only son, the scissor-sharp academic, who's lived for years in another, much colder state whose name she can't now recall. Long ago—a different world, a different life—the boy who went by his name hung in her arms after a bad fall and said "I love you" through his tears. A beautiful moment, but one long since buried under an avalanche of vitriol.

"Your parish priest, the good and gregarious saint of St. Stephen's—"

Nora swallows. With her bad eyes, she can make out only the chill blankness of her freezer door. "What happened? Is he . . . has there been an accident?"

"He is in jail. Arrested for . . . are you ready?"

Her brain fogs; the last words refuse to be clear to her.

"Perversion!"

Nora takes the phone away from her ear and stares into the mouth piece, as if the problem with the news is really some glitch in the apparatus. All those dots—the prick-like holes. Maybe they've blurred meaning like the AMD has smudged her sight.

"Mother, I nailed it! For years, I told you there was something not quite right about that man."

"I have . . . I have a bad connection," she says, hanging up, hiding the holes and the sickening words that fumed through them. There's solace somewhere, solace, yes, where it's been for years, in the evening routine ahead of her: chamomile tea, a home hunt show, a wedge of blueberry pie from Meals on Wheels.

But Nora is suddenly faint. She sags into the small nook in the kitchen, unable to imagine the strength she'll need to fill the kettle with water, to unwrap the pie from its plastic covering. Waves of silence crash into the room from every direction. She stares out the black window until visions of her son begin to shimmer on the glass: Luke as the bitter teen, arms crossed, face full of gleeful mockery; Luke as the sharp young man, running away to college with the sole intent of stockpiling arguments against the Church, against God, against anything and everything that gives meaning to what remains of Nora's dim world.

"The whole thing's bullshit," he told her the week of his college graduation. "A dumb Disney movie!"

"How dare you say—"

"'It's only because of their stupidity that they're able to be so sure of themselves.'"

"What? What? What are you talking about?"

"Kafka, mother. That's Franz Kafka."

"I can't believe who you've become," she said.

"And I can't believe who you are! Why, why, why are so many people hell bent on chaining themselves down to some asinine idea the first chance they get? It's so embarrassingly perverse!" His hands shook in the air, and if her neck had happened to be nearby, she thought that he might have choked her to death.

Nora feels for the knob of the small TV on the kitchen table, and sits in a daze until she hears the news for herself: "A popular local priest was arrested earlier today for propositioning an undercover cop." The female anchor—Nora can only guess what the young tart looks like—speaks in a tone that suggests the whole episode is vaguely comical, a close cousin to that News of the Weird her husband liked to read on the Internet. The anchor breaks to a reporter on location, a deep-voiced man who says that the priest, "trusted by so many," may have engaged in such behavior for months or even years. The reporter has been able to talk to a few parishioners, one of whom said, "This is not the man I know. Something does not add up." With odd ebullience, the reporter "throws it back" to Brittney, who promises "developments" as they occur.

Nora turns off the TV and recalls the last time she saw Fr. Hamblin, three weeks ago, when she asked Mrs. Haddad, the young widow next door, for a ride to church. There'd been a baptism, and Nora, still recovering from a cold, had to sit for a time in the pew. But she held on, buoyed by the beads of her rosary and by the thought of chatting with Fr. Hamblin in the line after mass.

"Ah, Mrs. Nora Ashley," said the priest in bad brogue, teeth beaming, sandwiching her fingers between moist, stove-cozy hands. To what do I owe this infrequent surprise?"

"You're the one who's been a stranger," she said, gently chastising him for not coming for dinner, or for even a quick cup of tea.

"It's true," he said with a hearty laugh. "Nobody's stranger than me!"

As Mrs. Haddad helped her down the stairs, Nora continued to bask in the glow of this hackneyed badinage.

"Are you okay?" the young woman asked, adjusting her sleeping daughter on her hip. "You don't look well."

Nora smiled. Words, she discovered quite late in life, did not have to be new, as long as they were kind, presented in this pillow-soft tone, which lifted her, which gave her strength to get through that day's shivery mist and rain. And maybe, just maybe, Fr. Hamblin, feeling guilty for his negligence, would call her later to say, "Put the kettle on, dear—I'm on my way."

Depressed, feeling inside her bones the abject hollowness of things, Nora skips her routine comforts and goes straight to bed. Sleep, however, is a total stranger. In the darkness, she is reminded of the confessional—a swath of deep space, a frightening nowhere if it weren't for the ruddy turned cheek of Fr. Hamblin through the screen.

"Father," she said once in her early years of marriage, feeling silly with holiday glee. "What if we pretended our tiny boxes were reversed?"

Through the square mesh window, she could see the halo of a smile. "You know we can't do that."

"Hello there my son, why don't you tell me your sins?"

There was a long pause. She saw him move a handkerchief to his forehead.

"You know who I am."

"I do."

"I can keep a secret."

"Being a priest . . . is hard."

"Tell me one sin."

"It's a life I would not choose again."

"What life?"

"My life as a priest."

"And is that what you call a sin?"

"No, my dear Nora. It's worse: it's a simple fact."

For a long, long time, Nora tosses and turns and then she is not in her bed but in her dark, moist grave and time that does not feel like time passes on and on until a thrilling blare of trumpets and the earth above rushes in great gobs into the air and she rises from the splintering box, flesh leaping back to bones like buds to bare branches in spring, and she is up, up, up into gossamer sky, where there are triumphant cheers and a great joining of hands, everyone knowing each other, thoroughly and without reserve. Through the dense, parade-like crowd, after the brilliant ascent, she finds the restaurant booth boy from her single days. She finds her first child—a girl—who stopped breathing in the crib and she is—because with God all things are possible—both baby and adult, a comfort and a confidante even as there is no longer anything left to disclose. She finds her husband too—there he is at last, red face full of apology, saying he could not wait for her, taking her by his brand new hand toward an even brighter light, toward God, God as he is, God as he's been all along.

In the silence after waking, the dream clings to her with the ink-dark tenacity of absolute truth. If Nora could send it by computer to her Luke, maybe the words would blind him, knock him on his behind, like Paul, too busy licking lips on the road to Damascus to know at first the hand that had cuffed him to the ground.

Son

LUKE IS STAYING on the thirty-third floor of the conference hotel. From his window, he can see Boylston and Commonwealth and the rest of the fancy streets spreading out to the river. On the other side is Cambridge, Harvard Square, where Natalie has probably just settled on the T, those smart, sexy frames low on her nose to see the paper she'll be delivering by his side tomorrow morning. In a half hour she'll fill the eye of his door, smiling, head cocked, hair down, lovely in a black cocktail dress, and he will resist the temptation to take her then and there because what is the point of pleasure when you enjoy it without delay?

Luke goes to the desk, unscrews the cap from the fifth of scotch he bought earlier at the Shaws across the street. Returning to the window, he sips and watches tiny people scurry around Back Bay. The futility of human endeavor, he thinks, ashamed at the banality of the observation. But it is true. He's achieved so much: tenure, renown as a literary critic, a university award for excellence in teaching. Why have these things brought him more melancholy than joy?

Later at dinner, a glass of wine on top of the pre-meal scotch, Natalie like a dream of paradise before him, Luke feels better. He is a new man—powerful, confident, capable of exciting great desire.

"I have a confession to make," Natalie says, leaning in, eyes glinting like the light red wine in her glass.

"Bless me Father for I have sinned."

He smiles at the vault of his lover's brows.

"Oh, it's just something you say when you go in the penance box."

"Hmm, you have to go in a box?"

"In the 'olden days.' They tend to do it face-to-face now."

"As opposed to from behind?" she says, a twisty pucker to her lips. With Natalie, God love her, most talk tumbles bedward.

"Seriously. You just sit in chairs and talk. Like people."

"And why do you have to tell some horny molester all the things you've done?"

Luke laughs. "I . . . they're not all . . . I haven't. Not for many happy years."

When he was growing up, his mother would go to confession with that pervert Hamblin every Saturday afternoon and return home an hour later, the happiest he'd seen her all week, to make dinner—always something special like chicken in mushroom sauce or sometimes his favorite: salmon casserole. He'd loved those evenings, when mother, typically so despondent, so tired, so short with his weak-willed father, was as bright and lovely as someone a third her age.

"So . . . would you like to hear my confession?"

Luke leans back in his chair and gives her his most priest-like nod.

"I think I like you . . . a lot." She quickly sips her wine to hide the blush.

Luke smiles, thrilled as a pimply teen by those girlish words. He's forty-five—nineteen years older than this vision before him—but he feels the need to give her something back: a heartfelt disclosure, a truth that is equivalent if not identical. He could admit that he asked Natalie to be on the panel for New Orleans the year before because he'd become smitten with a picture of hers he discovered online. On a lark, he shot off a blithe email invitation to which she, within minutes, responded with exuberance. When he met her at the conference, he was shocked to see how much more beautiful she was than the photograph suggested. He sat beside her, amazed by how pre-presentation bubbliness gave way to an impassioned analysis of an out-of-print novel about a long distance swimmer who breaststrokes her way to self-discovery. In twenty minutes, he'd come to want her—both body and mind. Afterward, there were drinks and a late dinner and from her a tipsy profusion of compliments about his scholarship that first embarrassed then emboldened him to ask her up to his room. Later, after the frenzied start and finish, he marveled at how easy it had been to get from the night all that he had wanted. How easy—how quick—it had been to become someone else.

If he told her this now, Natalie, up to now a wonderful sport, might well fling wine in his face. At the very least, she'd storm out of this restaurant, refusing forever to see his story as the compliment it was meant to be. As she speaks with some anxiety about a tiny snag in her dissertation, Luke feels the burden of this secret press down on him harder than the secret of Natalie he's kept for two years from his wife.

In bed this night, after another experience of sex so arresting he can't help feel that he's pressing his luck, Luke sits up against the backboard and watches Natalie snooze in the crook of his arm. He wonders idly about his wife—if she were another kind of woman, one of those crazy ones who, upon discovering his infidelity, would threaten to bleed him dry and shut him forever out of the lives of their two young children. On a lark, he imagines hiring someone to kill this wife, wonders what percentage of men have managed to get away with such a thing. He sees himself sliding an envelope of money across a table at a greasy spoon. He sees the hired man slide open his own front door and slink across the living room carpet to where she sits on the couch, back to him. But when Luke tries to imagine the moment of murder, all he can see is his wife—the real one, the anemic blob—in one of her big, dumb sports team sweatshirts, turning with a mouthful of snack cake toward the raised barrel of the assassin's gun.

He snorts. Natalie shifts and smiles in her sleep.

It is, of course, the other thing he's keeping from Natalie—that he does indeed have a wife but she is a haggard frump who, after years of infertility, has simply given up on sex. If she were a completely different person, Luke wouldn't rule out having her killed for the simple reason that he loves Natalie so much. That's a powerful sentiment, he knows; however, he doesn't yet trust himself to express it in such a way that wouldn't make him sound half out of his mind.

Luke tries to sleep, knows he must get some rest so that he will be coherent enough to chair his panel tomorrow, but he's thinking of Natalie, of a real future with her if he can survive the trial of coming clean.

A shower—that's what he needs, what will help him clear his head.

Sliding from under the comforter, standing up, air cold against his sex-moistened crotch, he heads to the bathroom, makes the water hot—hotter than either his wife or Natalie could bear. This is his own world, and although the steaming rain of water can usually shut down his thoughts, he finds himself thinking more about cleanliness: bar soap and shampoo, wet skin and lather, grit and froth whirlpooling into the drain. The metaphorical implications of birth, rebirth, the washing away of grievous sins. All the tired tropes, and the earnest introduction to literature essays they continue to inspire.

As he steps from the tub, Luke hears his phone vibrate on the dresser. Dripping, chilled already, he tip-toes into the main room. Natalie, her face in a pinch, turns and draws the comforter over a bare shoulder. Luke grabs the phone, retreats to the bathroom, and hisses, "Mom, Jesus, it's twelve-thirty. Is everything okay?"

"The Lord is salvation."

"If you insist."

"That's Isaiah," she says before a fit of coughing.

"You're a few days early for Sunday school."

"Listen to me. That's his name. What it means. Who he is."

Luke is disturbed to find the mirror above the sink fogged from condensation. But what had he expected? What had he hoped or feared to see?

"Have you heard?"

"Heard what?"

"Fr. Hamblin was released the other day on bail and, and . . . earlier this evening . . . he was found by Fr. Bonner in the priest house . . . in the bathroom." More coughing before a quiet announcement: "The poor soul . . . he hanged himself."

"Suicide. And that means—"

"Mrs. Haddad is staying with me tonight. We are, as you can imagine . . . beside ourselves."

"A mortal sin," Luke says, tempted to wonder aloud, "Despair or further perversion?" Was the good priest fatally ashamed or indulging in a little autoerotic asphyxiation?

"God forgives us all."

His mother is old, and yet—like always—he wants so much to be horrible to her. Instead, he bites his tongue. He puts a fist to the bathroom mirror and swirls it round and round.

"Luke?"

In the space he's tried to clear is a cloudy apparition.

"Son? The world is hard. It's not right in the head."

Luke nods. He recalls the title of his conference paper, in part a line from McCarthy: "There is no God and we are his prophets." He looks again at the mirror. For a second, he thinks he's left this earth. For another, he thinks some new self is coming.

"Where are you?" Natalie yawns from the other room.

"Son?" his mother says. "You still there?"

Luke looks down—at his chest, at his belly, at the sad, damp finger dropping from its nest to brood in empty space.

If No One Was Strange

DEAD WOOD. LONG, erratic hairlines twisting towards a black, bird-dropped dot. A cry. The gay report of laughter. Eve looks from the picnic table to see Olivia charging across the grass, tails of her pocket kite snapping red against the blue. Another girl—also six, maybe a year younger—appears behind, fingers firing into the air.

"Boy, is it hot!" Olivia says, reaching the picnic table, swiping hair from her damp face.

"Here." Eve holds out a thermos. "Drink some water."

"I met a friend. Her name is Virinda."

Virinda totters up—deep eyes, braids, bright baby teeth against shiny brown skin.

"Come along now, come along now," a man in white shirt and shorts calls from a nearby table. He approaches, hand beckoning. "You must leave those good people alone."

"It's alright," Eve says.

"See you!" the girl cries, running to her father, who drops an arm around her. Behind them, a short, elderly woman in a sari stands between two giggling boys and forks food onto paper plates. A family, Eve thinks—together, peaceful and content, enjoying an uncomplicated summer day.

In recent years, on the mercifully infrequent trips to Ohio to visit her parents, she and Jacob made it a habit to drive a long stretch of Route 30 to escape the criminal expense of the turnpike, stopping here in Bedford, at this thin strip of green along the Juniata, for a nice picnic lunch. Today, Eve has taken this back road for an entirely different reason: to slow down the day, to put the brakes on her arrival in Akron, the city of her birth, the place where (she has no other words) all hell has broken loose.

"Can I play a little longer?" Olivia drags pink crocs in the dirt. A light breeze ripples the tail of her grounded kite. Eve is reminded of years ago, during one of her father's famous rages, when she escaped to the backyard only to find a dying sparrow struggling to lift its wing in the grass behind the shed.

"Please?"

Eve is sorely tempted to stay here, to find a room in this small town for the night. There's an eighteenth-century village a few miles down the road, and she'd like nothing more than to step back with her daughter into a time of quilting and candles.

"Yes or no?"

"You really need to eat something." Eve takes a half-hearted bite of turkey wrap to demonstrate what needs to be done. "Fuel for your engine."

"I've got a full tank," Olivia says, zooming away from the table to a nearby tree. "There! You see how fast I can go?"

She looks towards her daughter, but her eyes find only the sun—a brilliant hole, a muzzle filled with a flash that's impossible to dodge.

—∞—

Eve turns from the slammed hatch to see the man in white. He is smiling, nodding at the Eagles sticker splayed across the back window.

"Madam, may I ask if you are from Philadelphia?"

"Yes," she says. "Just outside."

About a year ago, Eve returned home from an after-dinner stroll with Olivia just as Jacob was squeegeeing this dumb decal across the glass. A terrible argument followed, one of the last they had as husband and wife.

"The City of Brotherly Love!" the man says.

Eve smiles; there's no need to disabuse him.

"I am coming from Pittsburgh. That is not as pretty."

"Nice place, bad name."

As the man turns to admonish his boys, Eve considers telling him that she had gone to college there, had met her husband at Point State Park one spring afternoon. Jacob had been taking pictures of bridges that crisscrossed the turgid rivers, of a funicular car wobbling up Mt. Washington, of Heinz Field from a number of angles. Eventually, he aimed at her, sunning with a book on the fountain's edge.

"Picture's going to cost you," she said, playful before she knew it.

"How much?"

"Information."

He told her he was from the mean streets of main line Philadelphia, a senior at the Art Institute majoring in graphic design.

"Tell me something interesting."

He said he'd been a punter for his school's football team and that once, with a late-season game on the line, a Nor'easter blew a kick twenty yards back over his head and into his own team's end zone, where a rabid, mud-slapped pack of opponents piled upon it for the score that cost his school the win.

Eve sat up, placed a hand against her brow. Upon closer inspection, she liked many things about him: the broad shoulders, the kind, crinkly eyes, the self-deprecating smile.

"Where are you from?" he asked.

"Acrid."

"Do you mean Akron? Ohio?"

"Acrid," she said again, beginning to grimace now at the rapid fire clicks of the camera.

"Hmm, that bad?"

"Pittsburgh is hardly far enough away."

The man in white turns back to Eve and says, "We are traveling to your wonderful city today. In just four hours, my wife will be arriving at the airport."

"That's nice. Do you need directions?"

"Oh no. I have GPS. I know precisely where I am." He smiles broadly, adding, "It is six months' time since I have seen her!"

"Well, I hope you have a wonderful reunion."

The man nods, and Eve knows it would be simple courtesy to reciprocate with some family story of her own. Her mouth opens again, but even the simplest of words—like "my mother" or "my father"—refuse to come out of hiding.

"Yes, yes." The man waves. "You have a splendid day."

Eve slams her door, jumping at the thunder she has caused.

"Can I fly my kite when we get there?" Olivia asks.

"No."

"Why?"

"Yes. Maybe." On her third try, she steadies her hand enough to slip key into ignition. "I don't know."

Eve exits the park. As she leaves the town and picks up speed, other words come—not from inside but from out. They break hard like wind against her face.

Murder is one of them.

Suicide is another.

She opens her mouth and, like the wrongly condemned, swallows them whole, one gulp at a time.

—∞—

A few rollercoaster miles down Route 30, Olivia looks up from her Easy Reader. "Will I ever see Virinda again in my entire life?"

Eve finds her daughter's eyes in the rear view mirror. "Who?"

"The girl at the park."

"No."

"Is there a chance? A little tiny chance? She did say, 'See you later.'"

"I guess anything's possible."

"Is it really? If I wanted to fly like a kite could I—"

"Liv, could you let me focus on the road?"

They rise again and dip, pass through the intersection of a hapless town. There's an unexpected bend to the right, and a billboard appears, its message bold and black: "SPREAD YOUR WORD!"

In Akron, in a matter of hours, Eve will be inundated with all kinds of words—from her brothers Jim (the proud director) and Andy (the sweet protector); from rattled relatives and friends, many of whom she hasn't seen in years; from bossy, sharp-heeled reporters demanding statements and details. With the words will come equally distressing gestures—a bone-crushing squeeze of the hand, a hug like a pillow over the face. Not to mention the eyes, the unspoken questions that will fire at her through sympathetic tears: How? Why? Did you have any idea? What could you have done? They were your parents—your own flesh and blood; why did you hardly ever make it home?

Against such a barrage, she is sure her words—whatever they'll be—won't stand a chance.

—‑‑

Olivia has fallen asleep in her booster seat, with mouth open and arms flung out in a repose that resembles violent death. Eve reaches back, tugs at an arm, hoping to rouse her just enough so that she might settle into a less disturbing position. After a few moments, her daughter does shift, but the result is hardly an improvement.

Eve turns on the radio: vapid country angst, a second amendment blowhard, a postmortem on the NFL draft. When they began dating, Jacob made it no secret he was "a diehard fan"; for more than a few seasons, she did her best to play along. However, one afternoon last August, when she returned from the store to find him stretched out in front of a preseason game, something inside her collapsed.

"Gorgeous day," she said, setting bulging grocery bags on the floor.

"I'm working." He clacked away at the laptop on his stomach. He was in the middle of a freelance project that was bringing in extra bucks, but that was beside the point.

"You're watching a bunch of brutes knock each other's heads off."

"It's not just about the violence," he said, sitting up, eyes full of injury. "It's about the strategy. It's about the beauty, the art!" From a perch on the arm of the sofa, she decided to watch a few plays, the last of which ended with a player on the ground so long they had to cut to a commercial break. Two minutes later, Jacob called to her in the kitchen, where she was bagging red meat for the freezer.

"My hands are bloody. What did you say?"

"I said"—and there was a tinge of annoyance in his voice—"he walked off under his own power."

To be fair, Jacob had his good qualities: he worked extremely hard, was slow to anger, had moments of great inspiration in the bedroom. When Olivia was born, he became a doting father. However, as time went on, the passion for football seemed to blot out everything else. Jacob began a new tradition of having game days at his house. Every Sunday, Eve bit her tongue as portly men in loose green jerseys gathered in the basement rec room to drink beer and gnaw sloppy wings and finger phones to check the progress of their fantasy teams. Before kickoff, they'd sing "Fly, Eagles Fly," a fight song that punched up the stairs at her without the thinnest cushion of irony. Periodically, when Eve was wiping the dishes or playing a board game with Olivia, a sudden howl from below would make her clutch her heart.

For the most part, she seethed in silence. Then, one Sunday evening, Eve said, "I have had it up to here with all of these weekend assaults!"

"Assaults?" Jacob said with a laugh. "I think that's a wee bit of an exaggeration."

"Takeovers, then."

"We're downstairs. We stay in the basement!"

The next day, when she saw Jacob—a father, a grown man with a respectable job—smoothing that stupidly huge decal onto the back window of the SUV, she lost it all over again. But the killing blow came a few weeks later, as she was heading out to meet a girlfriend for a cup of coffee and discovered latched to the back axel of that same vehicle what appeared to be a rubberized approximation of the male genitalia. Astounded, furious to the point of nausea, Eve stomped back in the house and screamed, "Take that thing off now!" Jacob did so (it had been, he insisted, a gag gift from a guy at work), but not until there'd been a full blown fight that ended with him hurling an open box of cereal at her, the flakes spraying like shrapnel against the wall behind her head. Afterward, returning from the kitchen with a broom, Eve discovered Olivia sniffling into her stuffed retriever on the stairs.

If her husband had to be a grown up boy, why couldn't he have brought with him to adulthood only the best of those youthful qualities: the sweetness, the wonder, the desire to explore. Why did he—why did most every other man, for that matter—have to drag along the bawdiness, the heat, the temper, the naked aggression? Why did he have to cling to that love of domination, of making people pay dearly for no other reason than that was part of the game? Why, in short, did he have to even just a little bit resemble her father?

Eve glances at her sleeping daughter in the rearview mirror. Jacob has been gone for some time now, so it's just the two of them. Daily life is hard—the drop off at school, the rush hour grind on I 95, brain-numbing insurance work, the pickup from school, standing in long Acme lines for milk and bread and other staples, throwing meat and rice and a frozen vegetable in a microwave bowl to make some reasonably palatable dinner, nodding off over a bedtime story, feeling always always always like the worst mother in the world—but it is nothing compared to the difficulties this trip will soon create. For all Olivia knows, she's simply going to visit her grandparents. She's expecting to fly into their arms and tell them all about raptors, the latest passion of her nature-loving life.

What words will Eve ever find to explain what has happened? How will she ever be able to tell her daughter the simple, horrible truth?

And when?

And then?

—⁂—

"Mom," Olivia calls from the back. "Are those people from the United States of America?"

"Which people?" They're in Ligonier now, where a sign for Storybook Forest makes Eve recall an old photograph of her and her brothers in front of a crooked playhouse. There's Jim, the oldest, standing directly behind her, hands at ten and two upon her shoulders. There's Andy, the middle child, eyes off to the right, hand on her wrist, as if trying to pull Eve out of the frame.

"Virinda. The family at the resting place."

"Do you mean, are they citizens?"

"Yes."

"Probably. Why wouldn't they be?"

"The woman was wearing a costume."

"That's a traditional dress from their country."

"But you said they were from the United States of America."

"Yes." Eve grips the wheel tighter. "But America is made up of all different kinds of people. Living together."

In her current mood, Eve wants to see the picture as the epitome of sibling dysfunction. As self-appointed father figure of the family, Jim has always hovered over her, dispensing frank advice about what to do and how to live. Andy, for his part, was able to on rare occasions overcome his natural diffidence long enough to rescue her from Jim's overbearing ways. But if she wants to be fair, she knows that to take this one image as the whole story of their lives would be unfair. There are other shots of the three of them jammed into a frame, falling over each other, laughing like crazy. These pictures—hundreds of them—are in a series of beautiful albums still lined up on three full shelves beside the television cabinet inside the sturdy Victorian in which she'd come of age. At, in other words, the scene of the crime.

"Mom?"

"Yes."

"Can I ask you another question?"

"I'd rather—okay, okay, go ahead."

"Do people on the other side of the world miss us?"

"They don't even know us. They're strangers."

Years ago, fed up after several long-time neighbors moved away or died, Eve's father came home from work one night and announced in no uncertain terms that "we're running out of friends."

Olivia frowns. "That's sad, isn't it?"

"Yes, honey."

Then he set down two guns on the kitchen table, one deathly clunk after the other, so everyone would recognize them when they saw them and "stay the hell away." Mom put two hands over her mouth. Jim leaned forward for a better look while Andy stepped in front of Eve to block her view. No matter. She could still hear her father go on at great length about these strange new neighbors—how they didn't have jobs, didn't know the language, didn't care about their houses or lawns or other people's property and peace. How they sat on front porches or gathered on street corners, waiting for opportunities. He cited a break in down the street as evidence that everything around them had gone to the dogs.

"If they step one foot inside the door," her father explained, "I'm allowed to shoot. The law is on my side."

A few days later, Jim, by then a high school junior, gathered Eve and Andy in his bedroom to say that their father had allowed him to fire one of them the evening before. He spoke with great relish about the stunning recoil, the soreness in his shoulder. "If he's not at home when something happens," Jim explained, face beaming, "I'm the man in charge."

"I have an idea," Olivia says.

"Okay . . ."

"What if we knew everyone? What if no one was strange?"

Eve studies a strip of chain restaurants and stores they happen to be passing. She has long lamented the sad homogeneity of American culture, but, depressed as it often makes her, she's beginning to think that sameness might be the one true ticket to permanent peace.

—⁂—

Eve's cell rings. One eye on the road, she burrows through her purse for the phone. It's Jim, reminding her that time, despite the winding back roads and picnic stops, is moving forward at the same appalling pace as always.

"Where are you?" he demands.

If Eve had taken the turnpike, she'd be nearly in Akron by now. "I don't know," she says, face heating up. "There's been . . . an accident. We're being funneled into a single lane." It's a lie, but she is surprised at how weakly guilt grabs at her heart.

"That does me no good."

"Three hours, maybe?"

His sigh is audible. "Look, Andy and I are at the funeral home—"

"Already? I thought you said—"

"They were able to squeeze us in today. Anyway, we took a vote, and the plan is to bury them together. The aunts and uncles are all on board. I'm expecting you can live with this?"

Together? Eve thinks, barely able to suppress a laugh. Side by side? Why? So that her father could continue in eternity what he'd gotten such a great head start on in life? How many times had Andy shielded Eve in his arms? How many times had Jim ventured downstairs, threatening to call the police, while her father, ignoring them all, rushed upon her mother, shouting her down, freezing her to wall or fridge with any numbers of "ought tos"—"I ought to punch you in the face," "I ought to break your legs," "I ought to shoot you in the goddamn head"? The battles were so similar and occurred so close upon one another that, all these years later, Eve finds it impossible to tell them apart.

"Better than blows," Andy would always say later, stroking her hair when their father stormed from the house to cool off in the car. "Better than blows."

"I ought to, I ought to," "I ought to." Who knows?—maybe her father thought his threats were a kind of benevolence. How often, though, had Eve wished for him to follow through just once, certain that a bloody nose or lip would be enough to stun him into kindness.

"Eve?" It's Jim again, reminding her of the present.

"No," she says. It may be the first time she's ever used that word with her oldest brother.

"Are you serious?"

"Why does he get to win? Why does he get anything at all?"

"There are no winners, Eve. Plus, the plot's already paid for. There's really no use wasting mon—"

"No, no. I vote no!"

"Look, I—we—you really need to be an adult about this."

When Eve first told Jim about her impending divorce, the first thing he said was, "Why couldn't you be more accommodating?" He used his own marriage as an example. There'd been some bumps and bruises, sure, but he and Janey had been together for sixteen years. "Sixteen years and counting." Eve nodded, but she had to bite her cheeks to keep from laughing. As if counting was the way to measure love! Andy, in contrast, had responded to her news in his usual diplomatic way. Whatever honest feeling he had about the matter was disguised behind the bland observation, "It's just so sad when things don't work out."

All this time later, she's still not sure which response was worse.

"Eve? Evie? Are you with us?" Jim's voice is hard, a hand shaking her shoulder.

She desperately wants not to give into her brother, but really, what right does she have to resist? For years, Jim had shouldered nearly the entire burden of caring for their parents: buying groceries, picking up prescriptions, cleaning the gutters, even painting the peak of the house every few years. He'd been the one who kept the two of them in occasional contact with the outside world.

And, of course, he'd been the one who discovered the bodies. In a surprisingly controlled voice on the phone yesterday afternoon, he'd explained to Eve how he'd stopped over during his lunch break to mow the lawn and entered, as usual, with his key. He was looking down at a junk mail circular he'd brought in from the box—

"Oh God, don't . . ." Eve cried.

"No. Be quiet. Listen to me." Jim, seizing on the moment to underscore his authority, went on to say that he looked up from the circular to see their mother where she'd never been before—on the kitchen floor, eyes open, newly permed hair resting on a blanket of blood. On the placemat by her chair was a glass of diet cola and a mound of untouched cottage cheese. He found their father upstairs on the toilet seat, pants at his ankles, a "smear of bone and brain against the wall" Jim had just painted for them the month before. "I knew it would happen," he went on, voice vibrating with anger, grief, and pride. "I called it. Goddamn, I called it!"

All those years and all those threats, yet her father had never (to her knowledge) so much as touched a hair on her mother's head. He hadn't done it and hadn't done it; therefore, Eve concluded, he would never ever do it because, after seventy years, you are who you are. This had been the careful logic that protected her throughout her youth and, later, during those rare visits home.

"Eve, look, I have to go. We've got to do it this way."

"No," she says. "No, no, no."

"Be quiet. It's settled. We'll talk more when you get here."

Eve throws the phone on the passenger seat.

"Mommy, who was that?"

She wipes her eyes with a palm. "No one."

"Why were you saying 'no' all the time?"

"Liv—"

"Was it Grandpa? Were you teasing him? You should have told him to go fly a kite!"

"No. What are you—Why would he—?"

"Last time, last year, I came into the TV room, and he told me 'Go fly a kite.' I said 'I don't have one.'"

"It's just an expression. A figure of speech. It means 'Get lost.' 'Go away.'"

Olivia blinks at Eve in the rear view mirror.

"He didn't really mean what he said."

"Then why—"

"He was joking."

"Is that funny?"

"Yes, love. Now please would you let me concentrate on the road?"

—·m·—

"Mom?"

"For God's sake, what?"

"I love you."

They are on I 76, thirty miles from Akron, no more than a half hour away. A few moments earlier, the phone had rung again, but Eve didn't answer, unable to face another avalanche of words.

"I'm sorry, honey. I love you too. Why don't you close your eyes for awhile? We'll be there before you know it."

Olivia puts her head back and turns toward the window. Eve tries to calm herself with small, measured breaths, but the car hits an odd patch of asphalt and the tires thump like an anxious heart. She thinks of football—time winding down, the teams frantic to get into position for the next play. "Poise," Jacob had told her. That was yet another thing she was to admire about those who played the game.

"Mom?"

"Yes. Honey?" She closes her eyes for a moment.

"Are dark people good people?"

"What now? What on earth are you talking about?"

"Sorry…"

Traffic is beginning to build. "No, go ahead. Tell me."

"The last time, the last day, when me and Grandpa drove to the library, he said that every person gives you a sign, like signs on the road. There's Slow and Merg . . ."

"Merge."

"Yeah, Merge, No U-Turn, Stop, like that."

Eve nods. Brake lights glare at her through the dusk.

"And the signs have different colors you have to pay attention to."

"Okay . . ."

"And some colors—the darker ones—are bad. They'll grab you. Or shoot you."

The car rocks in a sudden wind. Poise, she thinks, gripping the wheel. Control.

"Was that another one of his kiddings?"

She takes a deep breath before saying, "That man was a fool."

"Who?"

That man. That woman. What had either of them been to Eve over all of these terrible years? Not a father and a mother but total strangers. And now? Two bodies already on the road to rot. Bury them together. Bury them apart. For all she cared, Jim could leave them out for the dogs.

"Mommy, what are you talking about? What do you mean?"

Eve's got ideas. Plans. They come in a rush, suffocating as a strong, sudden wind. She's going to get off at the next exit, put the car in park, turn to her daughter in her cosy seat, and fire several rounds of short, hard words to kill the Grandma and Grandpa she has been expecting to see. They were not your grandparents, she'll say. They were not your relations. They were aliens, creatures from a faraway world, a horrible rage-fueled monster and its weak and stupid prey. I'm sorry, she'll conclude, but all this time you've been calling them the wrong damn names!

And when she arrives at the house, when Jim strides out the door, moving easily through a crowd of reporters to take her in his arms, grandly, ostentatiously, in keeping with his role, she will let him have it. Andy will be sure to intervene—with gentle words, a calming palm upon her shoulder—but she'll fling him off. She'll splinter, burst, fly all over the place.

No, no, she won't. She's not made for confrontation.

Yes, yes—for once she will be exactly who she has to be.

"Mom?"

"What?"

"I love you."

The wind rocks the car again as Eve drives up the exit ramp. At the intersection, she turns on red, ignoring the signal swaying perilously on the wire. To her left, McDonalds, Wendy's, Arby's. She blinks at these fast food restaurants and, for a moment, forgets what state she's in. For another, she wonders if she's anywhere at all.

"Mom?"

"Yes."

"What are we going to do first?"

She should stop. Doesn't the first part of her plan involve pulling over right now to tell Olivia the truth?

"Mom?"

But it's so much easier—a dream, really—to keep on driving. As she lefts and rights—through the park, away from Goodyear complex, buying time by taking the long back way to the house—she wonders what would be the cost of going on.

"Mom? Are you okay?"

She sees herself shooting back onto 76 and heading due west, arriving after a day or two in a flat and straightforward land she never knew existed. She steps out of the car, walks Olivia by the hand through still air into a light-strung family restaurant on the old town square.

At a cozy booth, she pulls her daughter close and whispers, "Don't worry. Out there, at the other tables—these are your people. I'm sorry I never had the courage to tell you the truth." And then, before Olivia has a chance to ask a question, Eve ducks her head behind the thick menu, which boasts in imperfect English of everything under the sun.

Injury Time

THE BAR IS called The Doctor, and the requisite kitsch abounds: Time Lord figurines, sonic screwdrivers blazing in futuristic sconces, a three-D Dalek whose red eye draws a bead on Tristan's poorly sealed heart.

On the TV above, the last Cup match of the day endures. So far, it's been a clawing, scoreless draw, but now—it almost seems an accident—a Swiss defender finds an unmarked teammate downfield. He taps the ball to the field with his chest and maneuvers through three opponents before letting loose with a scorcher from the top of the box. The shot sails just over goalkeeper's desperate fingers, but caroms off the crossbar and out of bounds. The shooter, totally gassed, thumbs up his teammate and trots with resignation back down the pitch.

"Good run," a voice calls out. "Out of this world."

Tristan glances in the half-moon mirror behind the bar and sees an older man sliding fingers over his smooth, medicine capsule head. Their eyes meet; embarrassed, Tristan turns toward the windows, where, across the Prinsengracht, stands the world's most famous secret house. Inside, Ellen is lost in time, no doubt tearing up over the bookcase, the writing desk, the scissored pictures of dancers and movie stars stuck to the walls. Who will she be when she returns from this sad indulgence in the past?

The bar door cries, and a well-dressed couple appears, gravely surveying the space before settling with audible awkwardness next to the man with the capsule head. The woman—late middle age, at the tipping point toward old—is all bangles and silk scarves. Tristan sips his beer and listens to her go on about the joys of being back at last in Amsterdam, where years ago—"another world," she sighs—she'd spent the best three months of her life falling in love with Northern Renaissance art alongside Peter, the man with whom she entered the bar. She'll "never forget" that brown café on the Spui, where they and other students gathered to smoke and drink and talk like people convinced the future was theirs alone. And the Vondelpark—oh, goodness, the glorious Vondelpark! What better place in the world was there for wine and Geitenkaas and good, hearty bread than under a thick head of leaves by that sleepy pond, live Puccini on the stage before them. The friends had kept in touch on and off for decades, always with the dream—no, with the promise—that the woman would return to revisit with him all of their precious haunts.

"And Lydia, because I'm such a good sport," the man with the capsule head declares, "here the hell you are!"

"Darling," Lydia says to Peter, "in a parallel universe, did you know that you and I are in the midst of a long and happy marriage?"

Smiling diplomatically, Peter turns the subject to football: VanPersie's astounding header; the inconceivable pace of Robben; the healthy odds for the Dutch to win it all.

"The German side is particularly strong," the husband says, leaning towards his wife.

"See. It's him. He's always trying to get me—"

"It's just the truth. They're the odds-on favorites."

Peter squeezes Lydia's hand. He's a swarthy man, with meticulous black hair parted on the side, a melon colored silk shirt yawning wide at the neck. He resembles a movie star from the 60s. Tony Perkins, maybe. George Hamilton. A standard of suaveness that hasn't quite stood the test of time.

"Will you look at that?" Peter says, pointing to an intricate build up by the Swiss.

"No offense, but all I see is pure corruption," Lydia says. "Governmental greed, fats cats raking in millions, while the poor Brazilians continue to languish in all those crowded, dangerous, unsanitary—"

"Give it a break, Lyd," the husband says. "The whole world's watching."

"That's the problem. They're watching. Three hundred million, five hundred million—whatever the number is—everyone's complicitous."

The bells from the Westerkerk begin their melodic tumble. Tristan looks back out the windows at the famous house, in front of which a line of tourists still stands. Yesterday morning, a teen in heels and mini skirt trying to snap a picture of the place stepped back, back, back—and right into the canal. Out to walk off one of Ellen's soul-destroying glooms, Tristan had watched it all unfold, shocked at first by the girl's obliviousness and then, as bystanders scrambled to the rescue, secretly pleased by her choking sobs, the way her blouse sagged like a ghost from her shoulders as she was pulled from the water. It was a lesson in perspective—a stiff, swift punishment for a moment's inattention.

"Did you know," the husband says, "it wasn't just the Jews."

"What on earth are you talking about?"

"The Germans—they suffered too. After the war, the Poles, the Czechs, they packed them on trains, sent them to camps. Prettied things up by calling the whole thing 'Relocation.'"

Lydia sighs. "I'm not going to sit here and listen to your revisionist—"

"It happened! They put Germans in Auschwitz, for Christ's sake. Two weeks after it was liberated. Tell me, does the name Auschwitz mean anything to you?"

"Fine," Lydia says after a moment of silence. "Poetic justice."

"Men, women across the country—they starved to death . . . if they weren't shot dead on the spot by some ignorant, power-crazed guard. These victims were good Germans, mind you—Germans who couldn't stand the Nazis, who in many cases actively resisted the Reich. It's true. All you have to do is look it up."

"Are you finished? She glances down at the empty glasses in front of him. "You sure look to me like you're finished."

"And let's not forget—let's never forget—the children," the husband says, striking the table with an open hand. "Innocent German kids who came home from school or the store to find their parents gone forever. And then there were the really unlucky ones—infants tossed off cliffs, babies on trains who froze to death in pools of piss . . ."

Tristan closes his eyes to the laser of pain that begins to burn into his chest.

"You said you would be good. You haven't been for years, but—"

"Lydia, dear, I was under the impression that you had a heart."

"One thing I know for sure. This is the closest I'll ever come. You'll never in this life or the next get me to step one foot into that Godforsaken land."

"We should probably stop speaking for a while," Peter says, eyes nervously darting around the bar. "After all, there are people—"

"People? People? You mean like this amiable young fellow?" In the mirror, Tristan sees the husband throw his drink through the hole in his prescription capsule head. "Perhaps this fine young lad would like to pull up a chair?"

"I'm good," Tristan says. "But thank you."

"Drowning sorrows or counting all your blessings?"

"Oh, I'm . . . I'm just waiting on my wife."

"Your wife?" The husband's wink carries the impact of a punch. "Ha, make a break while you have the chance!"

"What my dear husband has never understood is that relationships are hard work."

"Arbeit macht frei!" the husband bellows, fist upon the table.

Lydia closes her eyes, but Peter already has the man on his feet.

"Arbeit macht frei!"

A bartender in steampunk attire steps from behind beer taps to say, "Sir, it's time for you to go."

Spewing expletives, the husband caroms off an empty table. With Peter's hand hard against his back, he disappears out the door.

Tristan takes slow, deep breaths. With Ellen nowhere in sight, he signs for another beer and heads to the restroom. "Doctors," says one phone booth-shaped door, "Companions" the other. The show's fanatics might quibble, but the difference is clear enough.

He's disappointed that there's nothing special behind the door: no ludicrously archaic control panel, no gear or lever or button that will whisk him to another place or time. Just tile like a locker room shower, a floor to face mirror, a single malodorous stall. Over the toilet is a curled poster of the famous police box whirlpooling through space, and all Tristan can think about is the piss-poor special effects of the program in its earlier incarnations. At the sink, he punches the arm of the soap dispenser and is reminded of the Daleks, the longtime enemy of the Doctor. For the life of him, he can't recall the thing they loved to say when zooming in for the kill.

On his way back, Tristan notices a distinct change in the atmosphere of the bar. The lights have been lowered, and there is now music—loud, synthy, effervescent. A young woman with a sleek helmet of platinum blonde hair crosses shiny legs in front of him and, for a few precious seconds, he's twenty-two again—unattached, unburdened, trying to catch a pretty eye with a smile. Like everyone around him, though, the woman's caught up in the pulsing present, oblivious to his passing. By the time he takes his seat again, he feels like a piece of meat lodged in the long, narrow throat between now and then.

Sipping his new beer, Tristan watches the soccer match slip into injury time.

"You know," a voice from behind calls out. "You look a bit like my husband."

Tristan turns into Lydia's smile—a sad mix of coyness and solemnity.

"This is years ago," she explains, voice rising over the music. "When he had hair and basic human decency."

He smiles politely and looks back toward the screen, where a Swiss player is flying over the leg of a sliding Swede. The player goes down, rolls for several feet, and grabs desperately at his ankle.

"Sit with me," she calls out. "Make me young again!"

Tristan glances outside. Peter and the husband are nowhere to be seen. Lights twinkle on the bridge over the canal, but the façade of the secret house has sunk into the darkness.

"Or not." Lydia adjusts her scarf, bunching it beneath her chin. Her face is tan, the skin melty under a deteriorating base.

"I'm sorry. I don't mean to be—"

"I lost eleven relatives: grandparents, uncles, cousins . . . Margaret, my older sister."

Tristan nods. This woman is old, but too young for the war. She must have never even known this sister.

"You've heard of Mengele? You're young—a child, really—but please tell me you know who he was."

The Swiss player rocks back and forth on the turf, eyes pinched in agony. A number of Swedes surround him, flinging angry hands into the air. One nudges the fallen player with a cleat.

"Did you know he was in the habit of greeting the people coming off the trains? It was important for him to do the honors of separating the healthy from the infirm. You know where the sick ones went, right?"

The pain in Tristan's chest returns.

"That man—what am I saying, that devil—he touched my father when he arrived. Clapped him like an old friend upon the shoulder. Flashed that gap-toothed smile. Father said if that didn't kill him, nothing would. He was eighty-five pounds by the time the Allies arrived."

The referee shows the Swedish defender a red card. His teammates scream, surround the man to plead their case. He listens for a few moments before striding away, stiff-lipped and steely-eyed.

"I try not to complain," Lydia says. "I've had a pretty good life. A career, a house. Occasional opportunities to travel. Husbands, though—no offense, but it's all a spin of the wheel. We had some good years, especially in the beginning. Who knows why people change? Why they do what they do . . ."

The injured player begins to rise, waving away opponents who continue to jeer. Kick, Tristan thinks. Kick the bastard good—toe through the ribs. Show him what real pain is all about.

"I just wish he'd been decent enough to give me a child—someone to lean on, to team up with against his incomprehensible rage."

The laser burns again. It's working its way assiduously around the poorly sealed door of his heart.

"I'm sorry for going on. Do you have kids?"

Perhaps Ellen is done—perhaps she has just this moment burst back out into open air, smiling, brilliantly transformed, the past in a locked up room behind her. Maybe she's coming this way, unencumbered, across the lighted bridge. Long strides, a skip or two—the gait of a lively child.

"Or do you plan to? Forgive me for asking . . ."

The door to Tristan's heart falls open. Inside, beyond a billow of smoke, there is a cool, echoey corridor with several other doors on the left and right. And behind them? More doors still. Tristan sees himself walking, door to door, chamber to chamber, glancing behind furniture, peering in nooks, knocking on walls for secret passages. Each time he's forced to return to this waking dream, the place through which he wanders becomes larger and more labyrinthine. Hand to mouth, he stands in the main hallway and calls out his daughter's name, over and over again, hearing only the faint reverberations of his voice in return. Is she lost? Frightened? Playing a silly game?

"You look like you would be a great—"

"We do not have a child at this point in time."

"Well, don't worry, you're young," Lydia says, swiping a finger beneath her eye.

His daughter must be somewhere. It can't be possible that she's gone for good.

"You have your whole lives in front of you."

Tristan runs his eyes to the screen, where players from both teams drag up and down the field. He is tired too—exhausted, on the brink of collapse. What he'd give to be The Doctor, with a second heart for all the dead and dying of the world because, right now, there's no way that the heart blown wide beneath his hand is going to last him through whatever nebulous time there is to come.

Here Is Ware

Flicker Trick

FATHER SWEEPS AWAY Genny Cream cans and plops Sam on the butcher block table. Bare-chested, bald, he stands between her legs, which pour like skim milk from animal underwear. "I ain't killing you. It's just a haircut," he says, taking out his pocket knife. Beer, garlic, and motor oil—Sam wants to gag, but fear sits her still, lids crushed, dreading the jerk of hair, the move of blade through her precious strands of red. In the window, a box fan hyperventilates.

The trailer door bangs, and Mother, fresh from a garage sale spree, is a black lump in the light.

"What are you—?" she cries.

"Thing's sweating like a goddamn pig."

"Watch your language!"

Father shrugs, and Sam slides out from under the powerful stink of arms.

Later, a depression upon the bed, Mother moves spared hair from Sam's wary eyes. "Look what I got you," she says, bringing a ring from behind her back and slipping it on Sam's finger. "It changes colors, if you're happy or sad." Together, they wait for the magic—two minutes, five. Mother argues for a rim of pinkish-red, but all Sam sees is mud.

Asleep, Sam tosses to the flicker trick of dreams: Market, Bridge, Centerway—she hurries through the sticky streets of Downtown Ware, crisp steps behind her in the dark, shadows like fingers as she runs, and then a closing door through which she barely fits.

She turns, finds herself inside the long tunnel of a plane. No, she is the plane, a sweaty pink pig, galloping down the runway for the rise, two seething snouts for wings.

Shit-Don't-Stinkers

FATHER KICKS CLOSED the refrigerator door, punches out a beer. "Shit-Don't-Stinkers," he says.

"They're family!" Mother cries, flapping a bag at an overstuffed garbage can.

"Pen's your blood, not mine."

Ground beef spits and pops on the stove. By the front room window, Sam glances up from her *Little House* book to see Aunt Pen's hatchback lurch over a speed bump into the trailer park. Sam stands, hand tightening on her plastic bag of clothes.

"I'm leav-ing," she sings as Grace leaps from the car, blue eyes swimming. Mother, saggy in sweats, shuffles to the door for a wave. In the kitchen, Father forages with fingers in the pan.

Aunt Pen, Uncle Mike, and Grace live a long distance call down Route 13, half way to Horseheads. It's warm for October—bold sun, windbreaker weather—so Sam and Grace dart into vast backyard grass, hole up in the A-frame playhouse scratching summer plans on colorful construction paper: the Arnott Mall, Darien Lake, camping at Buttermilk Falls. The window is thrown open for a fine pine needle breeze. On the deck, Uncle Mike flips fat burgers. He whistles softly, points a beer at a doe nudging through the trees. After dinner, Sam and Grace gobble double fudge ice cream while melting by the wood burning stove. Aunt Pen enters the room with a flourish. She claps, asks, "What else do we need?" Sam smiles, shakes her head to say she's good. The evening yawns before her, wide and warm, her best friend in all the world.

Connect Four

CHRISTMAS AFTERNOON, GRANDA and Gramma's, the house stuffed like a bird with family: Aunt Leah, Uncle Frank (a week out of prison) and their thundering, bumbling boys; Uncle Henry in his transmission shop jumpsuit, Phyllis with her bangles and Jolly Roger grin; Aunt Jane and her most recent in a line of cover band guys, hands all over her behind, hell bent on adding to her unruly brood; Aunt Doreen, press on nails scissoring the air, going on about the adorable black lady who sells gloss and foundation on the Home Shopping Club. Later, quietly, a half hour before dinner, Aunt Pen, Uncle Mike, and Grace appear, risking a trip into town. Grace has barely enough time for a "hi" before being pressed into princesshood by the sword-wielding boys.

Sam returns to the kitchen table, plays Connect Four against herself again. Plink, plink, plink go the checkers. Red blocks black. Black blocks red.

Below, the men stride around cover band man's black Trans Am, sipping beer from NASCAR cozies. In response to a holiday disaster that predates Sam, Gramma forbids drinking in the house. Not that it stops the holiday histrionics—bloodthirsty emotions smeared across faces and fists; the streams of self-involved tears; the grandiose speeches, crude and incoherent; the shattered plates, the slammed doors, the go-to-hells and much, much worse. It's only a matter of time and smuggled alcohol before this year's show.

The turkey's resting on the stove when the men return, spreading cold and a fine snow of expletives. They're oblivious to the grim lips of Gramma draining potatoes by the sink.

Plink, plink, plink.

Sam, careful as always, is on the verge of another stalemate when, at the back of the house, there is a savage scream. She looks up to see Father filling the jamb. "Stay!" he roars, hand in the air between them. He disappears, followed by Gramma ("Lord, Lord, Lord") wiping hands in a towel. Sam waits, catching her breath, then peers down the hallway to where light leaks from beneath the bathroom door. Cries and thumps, a bestial growl, the back door crashing. More wailing, the familiar voice of Grace like Sam's never heard it before.

"Yes, 9-1-1, hello, there's been a—Christ—just a terrible accident."

Sam turns. Aunt Leah's in the living room, tight jeans and bony elbows, phone like a baby in her hands. "An umbrella," she cries. "My niece got poked in the eye. No, no, not poked. It's bad. There's blood." Leah swipes her face with the back of her hand. "All over the place!"

On liquid legs, Sam drains back into the kitchen. Below the window, her cousin Mac appears, stumbling, pants around ankles. Uncle Frank rushes forward, white hair whipping, thrashing doughy flesh with the black J of the umbrella. Mac falls—"I didn't mean—!"—to his knees.

"If somebody took half the energy to watch him," Aunt Jane says, appearing from behind, jouncing a foul-smelling infant whose name (or father) Sam can't recall.

Uncle Frank loses his grip, and Mac, on all fours, makes a break for the trees. His father gives chase, foot cocking, cocking until it flies into the boy's bare behind and the boy tumbles down the snow-patched hill, out of sight, toward where that sleek sports car rests.

The following week, Uncle Mike announces his dream job in Richmond. On the day of departure, he and Aunt Pen take Sam to Frills for a sad sub lunch, where Grace sips unsweetened tea from Styrofoam and hardly says a word. Sam talks about school—"Well, history is interesting . . ."—all the while avoiding the black patch plastered over her cousin's eye.

Later, back in the trailer's gravel drive, Sam lets Aunt Pen squeeze her half to death. "Come down anytime at all," she says, eyes shimmering. Uncle Mike nods, hands in pockets, gazing toward Virginia.

Sam watches the back of Grace's head through the window of the hatch. She waits for it to move, to turn, to give her the meager consolation of the blue that still remains.

A Spire

As usual, New Year's Eve is uneventful until the kegs begin to float. Sometime after three, a couple of sullen men arrive, and there are sharp words (about a bet or debt), fists and screams, a window punched, a bullet through the ceiling. Two days later, a strip of string cheese flicking like a tongue into his mouth, Father smirks at the eviction notice Mother thrusts in front of his face.

"Don't matter," he says with a shrug. "I'm out of here." In Binghamton, his brother suddenly has all the construction work he can handle.

"What about me? And Sammy?"

"Come the hell along. See if I care."

"I'm tired of moving. Just sick and tired."

Father backhands an empty box of snack cakes from the monstrous marshmallow couch. "Real problem is you're too damn fat to move!"

Mother's flabby arms drop. Her face puckers with a cough before she bursts into tears.

"Christ, now I'm supposed to say I'm sorry?"

"That would be nice."

"But every time I turn around, it's you and the TV, chips or chocolate—"

"You're never home! What am I—?"

"That's the way the cookie crumbles . . ."

When Father leaves, Nike bag over shoulder, Mother, a high school dropout, gives single parenthood the old college try. She finds a new place—a dumpy downstairs on the factory side of town. She makes meals—macaroni and tomatoes, Tuna Helper, scrambled eggs and Spam. She buys cream-filled donuts and sticky pastries because a part of every day must be sweet.

"Want me to read a book to you?" she asks. "How about a game of Trouble?"

"Mom," Sam says, shriveling her nose. "I'm not four years old!"

Mother is back to buying garage sale stuff—baby clothes, costume jewelry, doe-eyed collectibles, *National Geographics* because she knows her daughter is the kind who loves to learn. A few days before Sam's birthday, she returns with an ice cream maker and a smile from ear to ear. She sets it proudly on the kitchen table, and they watch it while eating a celebratory dinner of pizza rolls, celery sticks, and Thousand Island dressing.

The next day the appliance is on the counter, behind a stack of junk mail. A week later, coming home from school, Sam finds it in the front yard, capping a fat black bag of trash.

One late Saturday night—3:38 through Sam's bleary eyes—Mother returns home, reeking of whiskey, swaying perilously, a condemned building about to call it quits. "I can't be good . . . for you," she says. "Not right now."

So Sam goes to live with her grandparents, a mile out of town, where mornings are chock full of blissful routine: Granda's spoon tinkling in a cup of Postum, the gentle wrinkle of the newspaper for a better look, the chipper beep of the microwave, oatmeal and brown sugar, fresh fruit, talk between man and woman in a reasonable tone. Amazingly, a spilled glass or dropped plate is not the end of the world.

And then, of course, the not-so-blissful routine: two or three times a day, the phone screaming, and Gramma, receiver to ear before the second ring, in a timid, strained voice saying, "Yes" and "Oh dear" and "Let's see what we can do." Within minutes, she'd be buttoning up her coat and heading out the door to buy a cousin or aunt a pound of chopped ham, a carton of Pall Mall's, baby formula for the family's latest mistake. After she'd leave, Granda would crease a napkin at the kitchen table, head a hoary metronome.

Sam is determined to be an exemplary child, not for fear of punishment but for fear of being lumped in with the rest of them—the losers, the leeches, the pre-teen run-amoks. Her grandparents have nothing but benign smiles for her, but Sam imagines at night, behind the bedroom door, blanket above lips, they whisper about her, gird themselves for the day she'll show the world that, despite her best attempts, she's just like all the rest.

No way will this happen. No way, no way, no way is Sam's fierce, under-the-breath mantra that leads her to straight As, to washing the dishes every night, to mowing the sloping, root-veined lawn, to taking the trash down to the road. When Granda, a veteran of Korea, says, "Young lady, you're going above and beyond the call of duty,"

Sam squeaks, "Really, I don't mind!" I need this, she thinks. The this then this then this.

One Saturday night, as Gramma's shaking popcorn at the stove, Mother fills the front door, car key an index finger in hand. "Daddy's back," she sighs. "You gotta come home right now."

By the old Reliant, door yawning like a monster's mouth, Sam looks down upon the lights of Ware, the shiny spire of St. Jude's. She's not Catholic—except for a few months of tent meetings when five or six, she's had no religious upbringing at all—but there's something she'll call holy about the fine point that rockets into space, showing a way to go or to be.

Point of View

HISTORY CLASS, ANNE Frank, and Mr. Carlossi is making a point about point of view. "You know what satellites are right?" he says. "Buzzing around up there in outer space, taking pictures and stuff." He slips a translucent piece of plastic onto the projector's heated surface. "Well guess what this is? Anybody?"

"The moon?" suggests William Frist, a pink faced boy who wants to have an answer for everything.

"Close, close. You're looking at our very own Finger Lakes. In winter. Not so pretty, right?"

The image is dark, sprayed in places with a ghostly white. The lakes themselves look gruesome—like dried up lacerations, the entire Southern Tier a cop show corpse stabbed and sprawled upon a table in a morgue.

"And here," Mr. Carlossi taps his pointer, "is Ware, our lovely town of 15,000 men, women, and wonderful kids like you. All that human activity—every single one of us with our individual hopes and dreams, our complicated stories, happy and sad—and yet this place is pretty much just a non-descript patch of brown . . . from, you got it, another point of view."

Sam stares at the southern tip of the Cayuga, the longest lake, a crooked middle finger tickling the town, until she's flung face first into a dream she hasn't had for a while: she's a little girl, five or six, anxiously scurrying down empty downtown streets, flushed from somewhere, the long shadows giving chase, snaking upon her, poised to strike.

Sam looks down at her book for support, but instead Anne Frank tells her she's given up on her fate.

Sam stands, says "I don't feel . . ." and wanders unmolested into the hallway, long and cool and empty, the fuselage of that plane in her intermittent dream. She tells herself she is safe. Safe. She is taking off. She is in the blue, buoyant air, the engine snorting angrily in her bowels.

Suit Yourself

SAM STANDS BEFORE the mirror, admiring the line of her neck, the gentle bump of breasts, thick red hair over the freckly slope of shoulders. Not bad, not bad, but when she tries a toothy smile, she wonders if she's good enough to make Daniel Ring say hello—if, that is, he's at the party, if Jen has had sense enough to invite Ware High's handsome poet laureate. While she brushes out her hair, the bath towel slips; turning, reaching down, she spies Father by the window, frozen like a buck. Sam blinks at the dusk, and there are just the trunks of trees. She turns the towel into a tourniquet, pulls the closet door in front of her like a shield.

In the car, Father yawns at the wheel while Sam stares ahead,

smooths the flower print dress, tries to make it longer, thicker, stron-
ger than it is.

"Drop me here," she demands, the pavement scrambling under
the door she's opened.

The car burps to a stop. "Suit yourself," Father says, reaching for
the radio to turn up slide guitar.

Sam escapes, shifts night bag from side to back to keep Father's
motor oil eyes from oozing over her behind.

Jen's house is packed, her parents away for a race weekend at
Watkins Glen. She sticks close to her friend until somehow—late,
late, late—she finds herself upstairs, alone on the couch with Buddy
Graham, an angly, amiable boy taking another shot at sophomore
year. She takes a swig of his peppermint schnapps, frowns, and is
glad he doesn't offer her the bottle again. Instead, he talks comic
books. "There's interesting stories," he says. "Good vs. evil, you know?
Sometimes, I put my hand over the pictures and just read the words.
You know, so I can make the pictures myself."

Buddy breathes heavily through his nose, the explanation seeming
to have worn him out. Sam, sleepy beyond belief, closes her eyes.
Moments later, she feels a bug, no a hand—a hand—on her bare
knee, working its way under the thin skin of her dress. She closes
her legs, squeezes them, tight as a boa, but can feel the pierce of his
nails into her thigh. She thinks of cousins: Aspen, Brandi, mothers
both, high school dropouts, wadded trash in the convenience store
dumpster of life.

"Look," Buddy explains. "All you got to do is lay there. I won't
make you go backwards, or anything crazy like that."

Sam tries to make her laugh sound more coy than dismissive.

"You just make a little tent with your knees . . ."

On the shelf beside them, animal figurines rattle from the sudden thump of rap in the basement. Buddy looks at her, pupils gooey with desire.

"I'm sorry," Sam says.

"Suit yourself."

Suit yourself. First Father and now this dim bulb of a boy, offering the kind of verbal largesse that makes her want to punch him in the mouth. Instead, she lowers her voice. "You've got to come on out of there," she says, each word like a link of a sturdy chain.

"If you're sure."

Sam opens her legs. His fingers linger on her thigh.

"I'm going to count to three."

"Okay, okay," he says, the hand shriveling away.

Later, when Buddy passes out against her, Sam thinks: What made her think dress? What made her think she could get away with bare legs? Next time, all the time, she vows, there will be jeans, something dark and heavy—something coarse. Fire to fight fire.

Man

"HEY, MAN." "MAN o man." "Man sakes alive!" This is the way boys greet Sam in hallways and on stairs, thanks to Tony Whitehead, who, in a sudden belch of inspiration, started the whole SaMANtha thing.

"It's sorta like a compliment," Jen says, stabbing a carrot stick in a pool of fat free ranch.

A trio of dainty-nosed girls strides by, salads and diet colas on cafeteria trays. They're chattering about the Sadie Hawkins dance—what to wear, whom to ask.

"I mean, if you're into those sort of compliments."

When the boys first began to attack Sam's startling new look—

earth tone corduroys and dark plaid flannels, paint free face, home-cut hair like a sputtering flame upon her head—Sam wanted to cry. As time has passed, the sharp words have been blunted against a shield-tough scab of indifference. "You are most definitely the man!" Tony said in homeroom this morning, giving her a locker room slap on the back, the faces of boys behind him wrinkled with sniggering. Sam, with genuine pity, thought, how stupid, how small, how absolutely animal you are.

Jen watches a clean-cut boy shuffle through the cafeteria doors. "Why don't you ask him?"

It's Daniel. Daniel Ring.

"Ask him what?"

"To the dance! He's in my English class. Just your type." Jen makes goalposts of her arms. "Likes his books about yay big."

A boy like that—bright, erudite, dignified as a head of state—could never even see her from his clouds. "Dances are stupid," Sam says.

"Sometimes," Jen says, snapping celery like a bone between her teeth. "Sometimes, you are stupid."

"Is that right?"

"And stubborn." She presses thumb against nose to show her nostrils. "Pig-headed."

"Oh, thanks."

"I only want to help."

"Don't need it."

"You know," Jen sighs, "they're calling you 'dyke.'"

"So?" Sam stops herself from saying: "maybe that's the point."

Jen shrugs, slides a manicured hand back into her sandwich bag. Sam is suddenly envious of all those vegetables. They look so good together—fresh, cheery, full of color, like fun-loving friends for life.

Audition

Shadow Box—the stark, black and white poster greets Sam and Jen at the cafeteria door. "Meet new friends." "Explore deep family issues!" "Find out what you're made of!"

"It's the second semester of your junior year," her guidance counselor had reminded her the week before. "If you want to get ahead, you simply have to get involved." Sam nodded. She's known for years that life operates according to the law of the Great Either/Or: act or be acted upon.

"I worked props for a show last year," Jen says in her new know-it-all way. "Too many freak shows, but at least the cast parties were fun."

Working props isn't going to cut it. And besides, is stage so much of a stretch? For years, she's put on one self or another at school. So far, she's survived the savage audience of high school boys. What does she have to fear from an auditorium of actual people?

The afternoon of auditions, Mr. Fortuna, the drama teacher, the universally acclaimed "cool dude" she's only heard about until now, blinks expectantly from behind thick frames in the first row. Behind him, hopefuls dot the first several rows of theater seats. Eyes wait, stare, judge. When a girl leans lips into the ear of a friend, Sam begins to freeze. She can't do this, she can't do this—

"Loosen up," Mr. Fortuna says, hands and shoulders wiggling like fish to show how it's done. "Whenever you're ready."

Sam hides behind the script. She opens her mouth, presents each word of the monologue with great deliberation, a firm foot planted on the ground. One after another—each step harder, creating a deeper impression than the one before until she reaches with great relief the pillow-white void on the page.

Mr. Fortuna frowns, frames dancing up and down on his face.

"Hmm, not bad, I guess," he says. "But your anger has to be, well, more complicated. There's got to be fear and grief and . . . what's the other one I'm looking for?"

Zoey, a tall, elegant girl who's just had her turn, suggests, "Love?"

"Love! Right, right. Johnny, tell her what she's won! Johnny?" Mr. Fortuna turns left and right. "Where the heck is Johnny?"

Sam is annoyed by the laughter of others. Even if she doesn't get a part, it's become life or death for her to get this right.

"Remember," Mr. Fortuna says, "you're writing a letter in the voice of your dead sister because your mother's terminally ill and you want to give her some hope. Long story short: she's dying and you're lying. Now, pardon the French, how the heck does that make you feel?"

Sam closes her eyes. Earlier this week, Mr. LaBute lectured about the ice age, the massive glaciers ("two miles thick") that crept down from Hudson Bay. He called them "sheets" but that's too smooth a metaphor for Sam, who imagines not a sheet but the hot roof of a monster's mouth, countless jagged teeth, gnawing, tearing, opening up the hard skin of the earth to lay bare its liquid heart. As she reads the monologue again, she thinks of Mother, a blob of sweatpants on that chocolate couch, smoke spinning from her mouth; of Father, those eyes black with desire and disgust; the ceaseless arguments; the name calling, the moment-to-moment animalism of each. She thinks of moving with little notice from place to place; of soft-spoken social workers, with maternal smiles underlining anxious eyes. The glacier exposes everything before melting from the passion that fires her skin.

When Sam finishes her monologue, the theater is a tomb. Zoey, the elegant girl, wipes an eye with a finger. Someone's script bird flaps to the floor. Mr. Fortuna pushes his dropped chin back into his face and breaks into a wide smile. "Yes, yes. More of that. That person is almost the one we're looking for."

Pick Me Up

AT LUNCH, ZOEY says, "You've just got to come. I rented *The Fog . . . Invasion of the Body Snatchers!*"

"I'm not sure," Sam says, trying to find an excuse. "Horror's not really my thing."

Zoey smiles—bright full lips, royal blue eyes, brown hair like a gorgeous theater curtain. She unwraps a fastidious sandwich, tucks a bean sprout back under the slice of whole grain bread. "If transportation is a problem, my mom could pick you up."

A series of mortifying images burns through Sam's mind: a fancy Volvo pulling into Stevens Park next to a muscle car on blocks; the shirtless, angry-eyed men on stoops; the frizzy-haired and foul-mouthed girls on stroller patrol; Mrs. Kress nobly containing her disgust in order to shake hands with her frumpy mother in their smoke-choked living room; the burnished Jesus smiling upon them from the wall; the TV whining like a child with a dirty diaper; Father slamming through the door, Coleman cooler in hand, motor oil eyes sliding up and down the woman who puts her own dowdy mother to shame.

Zoey raises her brows, offering a smile somewhere between hospitable and coy. It's inexplicable to Sam—the heat of her new friend's interest. Whatever's going on, she knows she shouldn't let this chance slip by. "I've got . . . some research to do," Sam says. "Could you just pick me up from school?"

Creepover

Zoey lives in a Victorian gingerbread on Fifth Street, three quarters up what's always been known as Rich Ass Hill. Sam picks at her overalls in the back seat, afraid to face her friend who's talking about the play, which opens in a week.

"Samantha is so amazing," Zoey says, blue eyes glancing back at Sam.

Mrs. Kress laughs, kind eyes finding Sam in the rearview mirror. "You've only told me about a hundred times!"

"She's got what every actor wants—a place to go to."

"So do you," Sam says, face full of heat.

"But you can find it." She clicks slender fingers. "Just like that."

Zoey, it is painfully apparent, has it all and more: a finished basement; cable TV; a walk-in closet full of designer clothes and shoes; a maid twice a week; two model parents—amiable, hard-working, healthy, and successful. Along the hallway to her bedroom is a series of portrait studio photographs. There's Zoey with praying hands to lips in a communion dress; Zoey in her eighth grade graduation gown; Zoey on point in a leotard; Zoey dazzling in a strapless spring formal dress, a tall, impeccably groomed boy at her side. All down either side of the hall the pictures go, parallel to the shiny hardwood floor. Sam is reminded of Zoey's smile, those perfect rows of gleaming, guileless teeth.

The two watch the movies sitting close together on the frilly, queen-sized bed, knees up, backs against the headboard. Half way through *Body Snatchers*, Zoey slides down on the bed, yawns herself to sleep, leaving Sam on her own in the middle of an alien assault. In the final scene, a desperate woman looks for one human being who has not been turned into a pod. She spies a familiar face, the health inspector who first discovered the truth of what was happening. He walks robotically, devoid of emotion like all the other pod people. "Matthew," she shyly calls, thinking he must be faking it to fit in. "Matthew," she says again, taking off toward the man who turns, stoic in his trench coat, eyes careful, intent, gauging (Sam thinks) the risk of exposure. Suddenly, he thrusts out a finger, emits this awful alien squeal. The camera zooms towards the humanoid's face, hurtles into its mouth, an endless void. Sam covers her face. Next to her, Zoey sighs, skin soft as a baby's, face framed by the pillow, a pretty eight-by-ten of peace.

Imagination

MOTHER'S HAND IS a mole in a tunnel of month-old circulars. A coffee mug drops from the kitchen table like a suicide to the floor. "It's one of those gold bottles," she says.

Sam bends down to double knot her combat boots. "You don't need it."

"I have anxiety. A certified medical condition."

"It's called imagination."

"Be quiet."

"What'd I say?" Sam says, annoyed, her stomach still trembling. Minutes before, she was in the bathroom, face down in the toilet. It's opening night of *Shadow Box*, and Sam is ill because she can't seem to find the directions to that metaphorical place she needs to go.

"You're not so smart I don't understand you."

"It was a compliment!"

Mother throws her hands some more across the table. Coins drop, a pack of cigarettes. There's the cellophane rattle of bills. Father is gone again—this time to northern Pennsylvania to shore up a crumbling bridge. "Here," Mother says, drawing a fist full of food stamps from the mess. "Drive down to the A Plus and get some subs for dinner."

Sam draws back, like she does on school-day mornings, opening the shower curtain to a slew of roaches. Long ago, she vowed never to use the paper shame of food stamps. "I've got my show," she says.

"What show?"

"Um, my play?"

Mother picks up a pack of cigarettes, peels off the top. "Right, right. You want me to go?"

"No, I'd be too nervous." What she doesn't say is she'd drop dead from embarrassment. What she doesn't say is, "Why can't you just be normal for a while?"

"Daddy's coming back next week."

Sam grabs her coat by the door. "You going to throw him a party?"

"Don't be smart." Mother lights the cigarette, waves away the noxious white flower of smoke. "You know, a long time ago—before you—your father was, he made me feel so—"

"I've got to go." Sam slams the door to the story of Mother's life. She thunders down the stairs, and of course—of course—the old Reliant doesn't start. She slouches in the seat, appreciates the irony for exactly three seconds before climbing out and kicking closed the door.

Behind the translucent curtain, Mother puffs her cigarette until a cough catches her by surprise. She cups her face with the free hand to catch all the ones that follow.

It's two miles to school, and Sam, coat zipped to chin, begins to walk. The further she gets from the apartment, the more her mind clears. Slowly, with some difficulty, she gropes her way back to her lines. She'll be late for call, and Mr. Fortuna will be upset, but once on stage, the ice age will begin. The frozen sheet will drop and sink its sharp teeth in. It'll leave behind the long hot jagged holes from which her transformed self will pour, the audience stunned before the powerful, magmatic flood. Afterward, Mr. Fortuna will greet her in the wings, frames charmingly askew, a "heck yeah!" burbling from his lips.

The Golden Egg

"RIGHT ON TIME!" exclaims Mrs. Sansevere, stepping from behind the counter, smile white as a wedding gown. The woman is maybe fifty—trim, shapely calves, heels, the red silk scarf a splash of sophistication that Sam could never pull off. As she shows Sam the ropes, Mrs. Sansevere goes on about her husband, a bigwig at Ware General, and her daughter, a junior at St. Jude's and an all-state everything. Sam, self-conscious in her first skirt in a year, feels what she'd tamped down earlier this morning: dread, despair, inadequacy. Not for the first time, she has half a mind to step aside for the better-gened and circumstanced; she remembers, however, that she was the one who'd been hired for the job. It won't be easy, but she will play the role of the young and plucky red-headed girl who belongs in this affluent world to which she's been invited.

"What's your favorite subject?" Mrs. Sansevere asks.

"Well, I'm interested in history. Local history especially. The Southern Tier. You know, how we've all got to where we are."

"Fascinating, just lovely. So how did you get here?"

"I'm sorry?"

Mrs. Sansevere laughs, stepping up into the stage of the front window. "Tell me about your family."

Caught by surprise but determined to do everything asked of her, Sam makes up a stumbling story about her parents: high school sweethearts, her father a, a project manager, a freelance consultant for some residential developer in Binghamton; her Mother a homemaker, career in . . . public relations happily on hold to make time for the "single most important vocation in the world." Busy arranging stuffed bears for a window picnic scene, Mrs. Sansevere "ums" her approbation. It's a mercy she doesn't press.

Minutes before the store opens, Sam pours a few gourmet dips, shakes multicolored corn chips into bowls made by local artisans. Soon, the wine and cheese types trickle in to graze, to marvel, to buy pricey, sensuous vases for Manhattan friends and relatives. Sam smiles, diffidently pushes peach salsa, which is only 6.99 a jar.

"Oh," a bangled, bare-shouldered woman cries, pushing sunglasses back into platinum blonde hair. "Isn't this a treat!"

Sam nods, smiles brightly. "We've got many more flavors in the back."

When the chips run out, Sam shakes more into the bowls. She rings up customers, recommends quaint places for a local color lunch. At work, she feels happy, productive, a special someone on a first-class flight to better things.

She Could've Died

It's almost like the holidays, except this evening, the histrionics come right away: Aunt Phyllis, more skeletal than ever, mouth open for moaning, hands hanging from her wrists; Uncle Henry reciting "Do not stand at my grave and weep" from the memorial card on his knee; Aunt Leah in a cocktail dress with plunging neckline and a slit up to her behind, blowing her nose with a ferocity that makes Sam clutch the edges of her chair; Uncle Frank in suit and tie, lying on the sofa in a sweat, his daughter Linda shouting in his good ear, "You

want to go to the hospital?" at the top of her lungs; Aunt Jane, fend-
ing off Cindee (her youngest) in an attempt to sob against Gramma's
shoulder; Aunt Doreen in bridal white, on hands and knees rolling
a miniature red Volkswagen across the room so two kids (whoever
they are) can give thunderous chase. If all that isn't enough, Mac, the
umbrella-wielding cousin Sam hasn't seen in years, plunges into the
funeral home, a desperate, "where-is-he?" look on his face. With paint-
stained pants sliding off his behind, he stumbles to the casket, falls to
the kneeler, and unleashes a primal wail. Sam moves behind a flower
arrangement and watches the funeral director wring his hands red.

Granda is dead—the day after *Shadow Box* closed, the old, sweet
man fell down by the road, the mailbox open, red flag up—but her
grief is put to rout by a heavy fusillade of shame.

Aunt Pen arrives with Grace; Sam has seen neither in years.

"You've certainly grown up," her aunt says, a startling edge to
her voice. The face, which Sam remembers as perpetually bright, is
pinched, skin taut and shiny like shrink wrap. Maybe she's just tired
from the seven-hour drive. Maybe too she's just annoyed by the foul
smell of family after all these years.

Sam turns to Grace. It's been so long, she can't remember which
eye is which.

"You look nice," Grace says—a lie if Sam's ever heard one. She
talks briefly about school—a summer in Mexico, a developing interest in social work, volunteer hours at the SPCA. Sam nods, keeps her
smile bright, even though the words sound like a speech honed on the
ride up from Virginia.

"Well," Aunt Pen says after a lull. "Bring on the crazies." She draws
a deep breath and plunges into the room, tugging Grace behind her.

Sam watches, smiles, grateful to have an ally.

Later, in the downstairs lounge, she listens uneasily to Gramma in the middle of a story she's never heard before. "He went too fast around a corner," she says, "and we flipped, somehow landed upright about twenty feet off the road. 'That's it with the drinking,' I said, and he bowed his head, sorry as could be. 'You're right, Nanny,' he said. The next morning, crack of dawn, he walked right into the kitchen and poured the bottles out into the sink, one after the other. Guess he needed the night to think about it!"

Laughter. Sniffling and sobs.

"Then, while I was busy frying up eggs, he went outside, put the car in neutral, and pushed it right down the hill into the woods! 'Had to get rid of the car,' he said, 'to get rid of that old way of life.' She chuckles to herself. "'Are you out of your mind?' I said. 'How in the ever-spinning world are you going to get to work?'"

When everyone laughs again, Sam realizes what's wrong: Gramma is not crying. What's more, she does not seem heartbroken in the least. To make matters worse, Aunt Jane throws arms around Gramma's waist, squeezes out plump baby tears. From where Sam is sitting, it looks like her aunt is picking pockets. Sam grinds her teeth; she twists a napkin until it comes in two.

Ten to eight, visiting hours all but over, Sam's back upstairs, paging through a Bible (the only book in the room) when Zoey appears at the door, black dress and heels, a necklace of pearls. Mrs. Kress stands beside her, slim and elegant, eyes scanning the room. Uncle Henry straightens, rakes silver hair behind his ears, moves toward them with an open-mouthed smile.

Sam slides from the folding chair, slips behind the easel holding the thumbtacked collage of family photographs. From there, it's three steps to the stairs, which she takes two at a time to the basement lounge, the bathroom, throwing closed the door and slamming the bolt in place. Weak-kneed, nauseous, Sam drops upon the toilet seat. In the darkness, she bursts into tears.

She could die right now, if only she had the strength.

Twins

THE SUMMER IS busy off and on at The Golden Egg. The Ware Invitational, Finger Lake Days, The Great Grape Awakening—each event brings in the attractive, affluent hordes. Sam gets forty hours in July and August, takes to splurging three times a week for a slice and salad at Angelino's. One afternoon, a week before senior year, Sam's sipping ice tea when a fat shadow creeps across her booth.

"Hey girl!"

It's Brandi—between Aspen and Cindee, the second of Aunt Jane's alphabetical brood. She's somewhere behind eye liner and blush, voice filled with enough unearned chumminess to make Sam's stomach groan. Sam smiles, pushes out imperfect teeth because what's to be ashamed of next to this high speed wreck of a girl, sixteen and chubby with child, receipt for pizza like a lottery ticket in her hand.

"What are you having?" Sam asks.

"Sausage and pepperoni."

"Twins?"

"Oh, you mean . . ." Brandi laughs, gliding a hand over her belly. It's,"—she snorts, she shakes her head—"just a boy."

Sam wonders how many more nods she'll need to make this girl gone.

"I know, I know," Brandi says, pinching a pimple on her chin. "Better luck next time, right?"

That night, Sam's at the Cup O' Soul, sitting with Jen after being summoned from the quiet room in back, where she'd been reading with grim pleasure about the lesser-known horrors of the American Revolution.

"What's that?" Jen says, making a face at the book.

"George Washington and stuff."

"So, inquiring minds want to know: Did he cut down the damn cherry tree or what?"

"Did you know the father of our country ordered the annihilation of the Iroquois confederacy?"

"And what about those teeth?"

"General Sullivan went through here—"

"Where?"

"All over here," Sam says, waving her hands. "Where we live now. He and his men set fire to town after town, chased away the natives so they could later die of exposure in the nasty winter that followed. Sullivan was Sherman before Sherman."

"Well," Jen says. "There was a war going on. The Indians should've picked the right team."

Two vaguely familiar hairdos bounce like balloons through the jingly door. They land on either side of Sam, barely acknowledging her presence. One of them—a Melanie Something—brings out newly-arrived college brochures. The three girls lean in, chattering excitedly about campus architecture, about Greek life and bar scenes. Huge, citrusy smelling hair bobs, encroaches, and Sam finds it hard to breathe.

"Colorado," the other balloon-haired girl announces. "That's still my number one."

Jen laughs. "Only you would choose a school for the skiing."

"I'm sorry. What again is the reason not to?"

Sam taps anxiously on the cover of her book. However, she's not thinking of Washington or Sullivan or the Iroquois but of Brandi, her pregnant cousin, born on the same day, a year and an hour apart. With no sources to consult, Sam is left to wonder what the girl might be doing now. Smoking on a stoop with a pregnant friend? Waiting in a liquor store parking lot for a fifth someone's older brother is buying for a price? Dozing off in front of Access Hollywood, lying alone in bed, unable to sleep, squinting into the dark to see just how little the future will hold?

The People Who Got the Shaft

Zoey stops Sam in the hall, beams that camera-ready smile, asks her to the movies. Jen phones, leaves playfully abusive messages, orders her to call back "toute suite." Mr. Fortuna encourages her to try out for *The Glass Menagerie*, says "I'd like to see what you could do with Laura." To everyone, she is polite but noncommittal. It's senior year—the platform for a splash—but Sam's new ambition is to slip in and out of these days without so much as a ripple.

Soon the offers stop coming, and autumn settles into its innocuous weekday groove: classes, classes, homework, homework, an entrée in the microwave and books about antebellum America until two or three in the morning.

At the beginning of the semester, Ms. Flores, her history teacher, declared, "In this class, we're not going to dwell on plantation owners, robber barons, military generals. We're going to pay attention to common, everyday people—the many, many people who got the shaft." So far, they've talked about the slave trade, the Declaration of Sentiments at nearby Seneca Falls. They've also spent time on the Second Great Awakening, the religious revival that "burned over" the area where Sam lives now. They've learned about Charles Finney, the father of the modern day freak show to which Aunt Phyllis—sometimes accompanied by Mother and Aunt Leah—takes all her "Praise the Lords." Sam is suspicious of such a man—his angry anti-intellectualism, his over-the-top emotions. Yet Finney was forward looking too: he dispensed with dour Calvinism and argued that a person was responsible for choosing whether she would be saved or doomed; he allowed women the opportunity to worship alongside men; he supported the noble cause of abolitionism. She's surprised to find herself touched by the description of his conversion. "I could feel the impression," he wrote, describing the workings of the Holy Spirit, "like a wave of electricity, going through and through me. Indeed it seemed to come in waves of liquid love . . ."

Every night for a week before she goes to sleep, Sam turns off the light, and on the blank page of black tries to tip even a few drops of this liquid love into her body. She imagines a turquoise vase, tall and curvy and glowing like an angel. Try as she might, though, she can't get the gorgeous thing to budge.

On Saturday mornings, before a full shift at The Golden Egg, Sam starts going with Ms. Flores to the Ware Historical Society. Here, digging for more about the fiery drama of revivalism, she discovers a treasure trove of material about Philip Anderson Ware—farmer, pamphleteer, traveling salesman, physician, and founder of her town. He too believed in God. He too had a vision, one that revealed to him the precise location of the human soul. If Ware touched it while one of Finney's electric waves crashed through him, then he could save others from the "final, awful, eternal separation from God." In a series of fervid sermons, he emphasized the precarious state of young women, many of whom were brought far and wide to him for intense "spiritual" probing. It wasn't long before he was exposed for a fraud and beaten like a dog up and down what is now Market Street. A few years later, though, the charlatan discovered heaps of gold in the West and returned to town so thoroughly a king that Onega became Ware within a week of his arrival.

Disgust, the best kind of delight, drives Sam through the archives: Ware's self-serving diary, the gushing accounts of his philanthropy, the hagiographic letters from guileless admirers, female and male. There are the daguerreotypes and photographs: Ware as a young man, hair charmingly filigreed about the ears; Ware as prospering divine, eyes looking past the viewer who is much too human to deserve attention; Ware as millionaire mayor—bow tie, vest, and top hat failing to disguise his corpulence. Over the weeks, Sam writes about the victims—the young girls good enough to believe someone who claimed he knew the truth. Mrs. Flores shakes the rough draft excitedly in her hands. "Look," she says, "I know you're a quiet one, but you are going to present at Regional History Day."

"No," Sam says, less a refusal than simple reflex.

"This is not a punishment. It's an opportunity."

"That's nice, but I'd rather—"

"Sorry, dear," Ms. Flores says, looking her in the eye. "You simply don't have a choice."

Please Go Away

ONE MARCH MORNING, Sam is at school an hour before first period to drop off the program for *The Glass Menagerie* that Mr. Fortuna had hounded her to make. His office door is closed, so Sam climbs onto the music room risers to finish up her Trig. She could do math all day. It makes her think of the stock room at The Golden Egg—cool and windowless, a world of its own without people or pain. At last, Mr. Fortuna emerges, cardigan and khakis, a mug of tea steaming in his hand. Sam thinks: comfortable—a man at home in this school, in this town. A man at home with himself.

"Ah, Miss Samantha Wayne." He takes the program, nods approvingly at the design. "You are a woman of many talents."

Sam nods, drops her eyes.

"Opening night tomorrow."

"Yes . . . are you excited?"

"Between you and me, I wish it could have been you up there, bringing ol' Tennessee to life."

"Something wrong with Zoey?"

"No, no. Nothing's ever wrong with Zoey."

Sam, unsure of what to say, chokes the mouth of her backpack with the fat math book.

"Decide on where you're going next year?"

Zoey's going to Princeton, and Mrs. Sansevere's daughter will be off to Yale. Jen—who couldn't care less about college—is headed for Penn State with the ambition of "drinking up a storm."

"I was thinking maybe . . . Elmira?" Sam says.

Mr. Fortuna makes a clown-sized frown. "That's right down the road."

Sam shrugs, looks away, eyes settling on a poster of the Estates Theater in Prague.

"You know, Mozart actually performed there."

An electric current moves up her back, spreading east and west across her shoulder blades.

"There are so many other places to see." Mr. Fortuna says. "You should really go away."

"No one in my family ever has." Unless, she wants to add, you count Uncle Frank and cousin Jack—the first back in prison and the second on the lam.

"You know, you could use a course in logic."

"I'm not—"

"You have to go away!" Mr. Fortuna explodes, frames going cock-eyed on his head. "No one wants to see your face. We're all just sick to death of it."

She smiles, grateful for his kindness, his humor. She wonders why he has no kids.

In on the Act Up

JUST AFTER MIDNIGHT, Sam slams through the door and nearly into Gramma in her nightgown on the phone, asking who the hell knows about how much money is needed for this or that. It takes a few moments to figure it out: Aunt Jane? Aunt Doreen? No, it's her cousin Aspen, nineteen and six months into pregnancy number two. Sam, dizzy from Jägermeister at Jen's, stumbles into the living room to watch TV and devour a cylinder of Ritz.

A commercial: slow motion shrimp falling, bouncing off a bed of rice, flakes of breading like golden confetti in the air; a slice of Texas toast pressing down upon a sunny ooze of cheese. Bright-faced couples laugh and gesticulate at a table of beer and burgers. A shapely waitress stops by, sporting bold, ecstatic teeth. They remind Sam of the customers that stroll down the aisles of The Golden Egg—wine aficionados, PGA fans, off-duty doctors and CEOs with houses on one or another of the Finger Lakes. Their mothers do not take government-paid vacations to psych wards. Their fathers do not weave serpent-like in and out of their lives. Their grandparents are not enablers, at the service of anyone ambitious enough to use a phone.

Suddenly, a technical difficulty. The problem-free people freeze on the screen, taunting Sam, making her seethe.

When Gramma hangs up, Sam weaves back into the kitchen. "How come you don't help me?" she says, mouth full of crackers.

"What do you need?"

"I need you to care. To, to offer me something."

Gramma zips coat over gown. She's still in her drab slippers. "Have you been drinking?"

"Yes!" Sam explodes. "I have most definitely been drinking. I've been bad. Soooo bad. Can you give me cash for a fifth of JD? Can you pretty please drive down to the store and buy me a pack of rubbers?"

Gramma places hands on the back of a chair; she doesn't say a word.

"Ha, ha, too late—I'm pregnant! Got a couple hundred to clean me out?"

"Samantha . . ."

"Save us all from another wild beast!"

Sam storms down the hallway, throws aside the door to the guest room she's using once again. She crashes to the bed, fingers clawing at the spread. Tears crouch in her eyes, afraid to make a break for it. From far away comes the sound of the front door shuddering to a close. Time passes. The text of her tantrum quickly becomes ancient history, but it sits heavy in her heart, a tome she must crack open before the school year is done.

Georgeous

GRADUATION DAY, A sprig of May sun through bent up blinds. Sam rises and sees a Hallmark card propped against her jewelry box. Inside, in a smudgy scrawl: "To my GEORGEOUS girl!" Sam looks for bugs on her arms, but she knows the bumps from wrist to elbow have been caused by nothing but those words, the creepy fact that the card had been placed there sometime in the middle of the night. She shudders at the image of Father in the room, perhaps pausing by the bed, running eyes up and down her body, maybe sliding a finger along the mattress, face moving closer and closer for a breath of her. An old dream runs through her mind. She rubs her arms until they start to burn.

Outside, Father puffs a cigarette by his Buick, unmade tie like a U-turn over the collar of his white button down shirt. She's never seen him so dressed up before, and for a second she thinks he's handsome. He spits at a sidewalk crack, and Sam grimaces at the gob.

"It's *gorgeous*," she says, impervious in her gown. She opens the card on the hood of the car, lines out the misspelled word with a permanent marker.

"What?"

"The word is gorgeous. G-O-R—"

"Are you, you know, one of them?" Father asks, waving vaguely at the red helmet of hair upon her head. The question tries hard to be a butcher knife, but there's something flaccid about the tone. He is angry, of course, but anxious as well, worried perhaps the answer might be something he won't be able to bear. Sam's scowl turns into a sardonic smile, which Father cannot see since he won't look her in the eye.

"All I know is I wouldn't put it past you." He flicks cigarette to gravel and clumps back into the trailer to tell Mother to "get her elephant ass in gear."

That night, Sam slips into the kitchen for something sweet to drink. On the way back to her room, Mother sits up on the marshmallow sofa, yawns at the real-life murder mystery on TV. "Earlier today, with that card," she says. "You know you made your daddy cry."

"You're kidding me."

"He told me at the ceremony. Then, when you came on stage and shook the principal's hand—you know what he did?"

"Um, he cried again?"

"He clapped. The man clapped for you . . . and, yes, he cried again."

Sam recalls graduation lunch—the three of them sitting in a taped up booth in the Seneca Diner, eating sandwiches with bland bread and faintly malodorous lunchmeat. Father looked out the window and Mother chewed loudly until he told her to shut up.

"Cake," Mother said when the bill arrived. "She deserves a slice of cake."

Father looked at the check and burned his oil eyes at Sam. "You want cake?"

Sam did not want cake. She had not even wanted the lunch. As she sat for that long and terrible time between the two of them, all she thought about was fall, when she'd be off for college, and out of the grip of this world for good.

Mother shakes a pill from one of her bottles, swallows it with water from a glass perched on her Bible. "Everybody," she says, "has feelings."

Sam shifts her weight and takes a drink of soda. She feels it run through her—refreshing, cold as hell. Together, they watch the TV, blink while the victim's mother dumps tears into her quaking hands.

Eye of the Beheld

THE SUMMER BEFORE Oberlin, all Sam imagines is taking risks, assuming a new self in some powerful, public way; however, when she arrives on campus—once her family is a good three hundred miles in the dust—Sam can't recall the role she's rehearsed. She keeps thinking back to a film in school the year before, at the end of which a soldier—a sensitive artist type like her dream boy Daniel Ring—gets killed inching out of a foxhole so he can better sketch a bird. A cautionary tale. For more than a year, Sam does her best to keep her head down, deathly afraid of taking a bullet to the skull.

On the rare occasions she craves human connection, there are always her roommates, Lily and Miranda, nice enough girls with whom she dines at Dascomb Hall. She spends much of her time in Mudd, curled up with a textbook in one of the white, hard-shelled eyeball chairs, every once in a while blinking into the room for a break. One evening, exhausted from an all-night cram for a chemistry test, Sam falls into deep, dreamless sleep. She wakes to a prod, the sharp corner of a book nudging her knee.

"Ma'am," a sandy-haired boy says. "The library closes in five minutes."

Sam, still silly from lack of sleep, laughs through a yawn. "Ma'am? Wait, did you just call me Ma'am?"

The boy smiles, steps back to run nervous hands through pretty hair.

Sam, stiff in the joints, tries to unfold herself from the orb without success. "Could I please have a hand?"

She scrapes her head against the top of the chair but emerges otherwise unscathed, surprised to find she's still holding onto the boy's hands, which are soft and warm like fresh baked cookies. She blinks, stifles another yawn, laughs again as they stand there, hands now safely at sides, the fluorescent light above fluttering off and on.

"Well, I'm Samantha Wayne. Or just Sam. Or maybe even Ma'am!"

"Yeah, right. Sorry about that." His brown eyes are rich, moist. "Timothy Holder." His voice is comforting—a stuffed bear nestled in a canopy bed.

Sam wants to stay—wants to just stand in his oven-warm presence—but the mawkishness of the desire is too much to bear. "Have a good one," she says, backpack over shoulder, walking past him with a casualness—an audacity—she can't quite believe.

"Um, Samantha?"

She turns smack into his smile, a force of nature that ignites his face from chin to brow.

"I don't know, would you like to get some coffee?"

"Chem midterm tomorrow," she says, pausing for effect. "I would like to get a lot of coffee."

They sit at a table in the Cat & Cream and listen to a boy with a scrubby beard strum Neil Young up on the stage. After a few sips of dark roast, Timothy settles down, becomes articulate. An English major, his passion is Keats: "Ode to a Nightingale," "Chapman's Homer," those intense love letters to Fanny Brawne. He talks about France, where he spent a summer as an exchange student. "Notre Dame," he declares, "was magnificent. Sublime." With considerable pride, he lets her know he's a Catholic, that he's five hundred miles from home and yet to miss a mass. Sam, reluctant to talk about herself, talks instead about the history of America, which she sums up in Ms. Flores' three not-so-short words—"contact, conflict, conflagration."

"That's a dark view!"

"And to think that religion is one of the main culprits."

"The Catholic missionaries were brave, men of tremendous faith. Some of them gave their lives simply for spreading the love of God."

"They spread their power. They hijacked souls. I wouldn't trust any of them as far as they could walk on water."

She knows she's performing, but Timothy seems interested in precisely this kind of Sam—independent, opinionated, hard-as-nails. Still, while he's gone to get them each a second cup, worry begins to worm; Sam does like him, after all. Just because the heart is the size of a fist, doesn't mean hers always has to look and sound like one.

Serious

FOR THEIR ONE-MONTH anniversary, Timothy takes her to Presti's, a fancy Italian restaurant a short drive from campus. "Don't worry," he says, "my parents send me a little something every month."

"How much?"

"Why do you want to know?"

"Because your discomfort is so charming."

He smiles into his iced tea. His face turns blotchy red. "Goodness, I don't know. It varies. Fifty. Maybe seventy-five or a hundred."

Sam hides her shock behind the menu, waits until it burns through her face. After they order, talk turns to the upcoming holidays, the foibles of family, the obligatory return to the fold.

"I have this uncle," Timothy says. "We call him—get this—Mister Insister because everything has to be his way. Last year, he made up these saddle stitched Christmas carol books for all of us. What's worse, he fancies himself a modern day Hal David, so he included a couple of his own. Wouldn't you know we had to sing the whole book from start to finish . . . before opening presents!"

"That's the worst you got?"

"What do you mean?"

"My family, let's see: What's the word I'm looking for?"

"Dysfunctional?"

"More like 'Subhuman.'"

"Oh no . . ."

"They're mostly about fulfilling their disgusting animal needs."

"You can't—what are you saying?"

Timothy puts fingers to his temples. Sam fears she's been too glib, gone too far.

"Do you go home much?"

She's been in college for a year and a half and has been back to Ware a grand total of once. "Here is home," she says.

Timothy reaches for her hand, mistaking her comment for a declaration of love. She's happy enough she's snared him; still, there's something bothersome about his gestures, his syrupy compassion, his desire to soothe in any way he can. Perhaps this rich boy simply wants to slum. Or proselytize. Get Sam to honor mother and father, love enemies as herself, chalk up another fragile soul for the team.

Twenty-One

IT'S SAM'S BIRTHDAY—THE last of the good big ones—and she starts celebrating way too early, margaritas and nachos for lunch with Lily and Miranda in Elyria, which somehow spills into happy hour with Timothy, who in between sips of Merlot purses lips at Sam, loud and reckless half way through a martini.

"Are you okay?" he asks.

"It's my birthday. I'm going to have some fun."

"I wanted to take you to dinner."

"Great, fine. Who's stopping you?"

"I don't think you're in shape."

"You my mother?"

"No . . ."

"Can't see you as my father."

There are more words, and all of the sharp ones are Sam's. At some point, Timothy is gone, and she's in a nightclub in North Ridgeville, North Olmsted, North Somewhere—colored lights swirling like her head and stomach. She's in the bathroom, Lily holding her now shoulder-length hair from her face as she spews red bile into the sink. She's in a parking lot, a boy in tight white pants moving like a dog against her leg. Later, her chin rests on the edge of a child-proof window, the wind blowing her blind. Then she's on her bed, topless. She feels around: alone, thank God. She snorts. She shakes with laughter. She licks thick nightclub smoke from her fingers one by one.

In the morning—head ablaze, tongue a furry animal—Sam stares at the ceiling, thinks of all she has to do. The phone rings, and Aunt Leah speaks awkwardly into the machine: "Look, I don't know if any-one's called you, but your mother's really sick. They did one of those biopsies last week. I don't know—you should probably call soon."

Sam swallows painkillers, a cup of burned coffee her roommates left in the carafe. She goes to classes, eats lunch with Miranda, and then returns to her room, where she replays the message from her aunt. Over the years, Sam's grown used to her Mother's dramatics, her self-pity, her chronic inability to be strong. But the word "biopsy" is new. Sam swallows another pill and dials the number.

"Cancer!" Mother says, crying into the phone. "Everything's over. The whole thing. I'm being eaten alive!"

"What kind is it?"

"It's cancer. Cancer! What's it matter the type?"

"Well . . ."

"You just don't understand. There's no future, no world. It's all going away."

Sam waits.

"Leah made me breakfast—pancakes and two fat links of sausage. For what? Because I was hungry. I'm hungry now. My stomach doesn't even know."

Head pounding, Sam holds her ear from the spatter of words. She doesn't feel much about being the most terrible daughter in the world.

The Art of Sitting Still

In Pop Art, Professor Stein lectures about "assemblage"—Picasso, Duchamps, Rauschenberg. Wearing sweats swiped from Miranda's drawer, Sam takes abominable notes—a name here, a date there, a word about composition. When the room goes dark for the slides, her eyes begin to flutter. Her chin falls to her collarbone and she dreams of Timothy—that sunny face, the earnest voice, the wholesome heat that steams from his pores. It's been a week since she's seen him. He's phoned once every afternoon, but she's yet to return a call.

"This one," Professor Stein says, "is intriguing." On the screen is a piece by Joseph Cornell—a nineteenth-century looking doll that seems to be sitting on a chair from which a number of strings shoot upward beyond the confines of the frame, undoubtedly to some out-of-sight balloon. Below the woman is a mountain range, snowy and spare.

"Is she rising or descending?" Professor Stein wonders, moving the projector up and down for a laugh.

Sam chooses B to suit her gloomy mood.

Stein shows several more works: parrots, owls and cockatoos; a series of jars filled with rubberbands, rocks, the wing (she thinks) of a butterfly; reproductions of a young Renaissance princess scattered between building blocks for kids.

"These are shadow boxes," he explains. "Collections of common objects in strange, unprecedented juxtaposition. We see each object in a startling new way."

Sam sits up, oblivious to pen and paper. *Shadow Box*—the high school play, the role for which she earned all that praise. Mr. Fortuna called her "splendid," wanted to see her on stage again. It was intoxicating—the lights, the speeches, the applause, the smiles in the lobby from boys who'd never before given her the time of day. But then Granda died, and Sam could no longer bear to be seen.

Professor Stein goes back through the slides again, offering more commentary. All of the objects are ordered, carefully subdued by the frame, the sheet of glass. Boxed in, inert, lifeless, there is nothing dynamic—nothing playful—about the contents. To Sam, they are depressing as pressed flowers, as butterflies skewered by pins.

Great Escapes

DEEP IN THE cozy eyeball on the third floor of Mudd, Sam sifts through sources for a paper on fugitive slaves. She reads about Henry Brown, who took half his savings, had himself boxed up and shipped by a friend from Virginia to Philadelphia. Twenty-seven hours he hunched in that container, by land and by water, jostled, tumbled, turned on his head. Must have seemed twenty years, a lifetime, but he not only made it safely to his destination, he had the spunk to pop from the box in front of a group of abolitionists and say, "How do you do, gentlemen?" as if the whole hard trip had been some sitcom lark.

The episode makes Sam laugh, lifts her like helium out of the eye and back to her dorm to call Timothy, eager to tell him what he wants to hear because she's pretty sure it will be what she wants as well. Face-to-face with the phone, however, her desire begins to deflate. She pulls a beer from Miranda's compact fridge, and then, quickly, another. It's the cheap stuff, bad and bitter, but alcohol begins to give the room a shimmer, a nightclub-like atmosphere of anything goes. She dials his number at last, swallowing hard between purrs on the other end of the line.

When he finally picks up, she says, "I think I want to apologize."

"You think you do?"

"Well, to be honest, I'm not sure exactly what I've done. I mean, we argued. Did I call you names?"

Timothy sighs. "Look, forgive and forget."

"Great." Sam waits. She drains the rest of her beer. "So, do you want to come over? Roommates are gone for the weekend."

"I would very much like to see you again."

"Just not now? Am I interrupting something?"

"No . . . no!" Timothy is mortified; Sam in her state tries to figure out if this is more good than bad.

"Well, I'm sorry." Sam is sincere, but she wonders if he'll believe this softer version of herself. She waits—counts one, two, three and still there's no response. "Timothy?" she says, her voice small, a child crying from a room upstairs.

"I'm here."

"Here is not here."

"I think I'd like some time to pray on this."

"Pray?" She feels the vomit rush of rage in her throat. Holding hand over the receiver, she takes deep, controlled breaths—in and out, in and out. "Okay then. Do what you have to do."

Miracle Cure

FRESH FROM THE shower, clean and soft, Sam drops to the bed and sends a finger down, down, down to where she splits in two, down into quick thick flesh, back and forth, a swimmer in oil, ready to go the distance. Timothy, she thinks, closing her eyes. Timothy between her, his smooth warm back a rink for her skating heels. Timothy sweet, Timothy kind—Come back, come back, come back—

The phone shrills, and for an exquisite moment she thinks her conjure trick has worked.

"Mom?" she says, trying to catch her breath. "How . . . are you?"

"Cured! The cancer's all gone!"

"Okay…" Last weekend—Thanksgiving—Sam dutifully took the Greyhound home, grinding her teeth all the way. There was supposed to be a family dinner of sorts—Leah, Doreen, obnoxious cousins and their kids; however, because Gramma failed to answer the phone the afternoon before, Mother refused to go.

"She was probably just out running errands," Sam said.

"No, no. She doesn't want death over for dinner. Who the hell would?"

So they spent the holiday alone in the dim living room, with lunchmeat sandwiches and cop show repeats, Sam holding her breath as often as she could while Mother smoked cigarette after cigarette on the brown marshmallow couch.

"There are, did you know, all of these super foods," Mother says now. "Oatmeal. Cashews, I think. That's all I eat now. Broccoli is another."

"Mom. Is there someone with you?"

"Sunflower seeds."

"What?"

"Superfoods. All you do is eat them. It's like magic."

Sam finds herself staring into Miranda's open closet, shoes arranged by type and color. Everywhere she turns is someone else's perfect little world.

"Salmon," Mother laughs, as if this is a game. "Do you know any others? I'm making a list."

"Cranberries!" Sam blurts out.

"Are they? Let me get a pen so—"

"I'll send you some."

"You will?"

"Sure . . . but I've got to go now."

Sam hangs up and drifts back to her bed. She studies her fingers, where the slick has turned in the air to something close to skin. Is it guilt she feels, this powerful shiver up her naked back and arms? She throws on clothes, bundles up good, and battles a stiff wind across Tappan Square to the co-op, where she stands for far too long in an aisle of shriveled fruit, trying to ignore the dampness of her eyes.

A Book by Its Lover

Timothy trails Sam as she works her way down a rack of blouses. They are at Goodwill, a new and not especially exciting experience for Timothy but one he endures in his earnest, amiable way.

"What do you think?" she says, holding against her chest a shirt the color of a caution light.

"There's something weird about wearing other people's clothes."

She laughs, lays the garment in the cart.

"You know," Timothy says, "I still don't think I understand you,"

"You better not." The reconciliation is still so new that Sam makes sure to add plenty of tease to her tone.

"I mean, by this point, I should be getting somewhere."

"Third base? Home?"

"Seriously. I want to know everything there is to know about you."

On the last day of classes, she'd been studying in her padded eyeball when Timothy appeared, crouching like a catcher so they could be eye to eye. "I need you," he whispered, eyes sincere without being too maudlin. Her first impulse was to make him pay with indifference, but the truth was she was moved. She didn't cry, but she had wanted to, crawling out of that chair into his arms. And now—now, she finds herself just a little bit unnerved by the renewed intensity of his attentions.

"I'm like a book," she says. "A cunning story. You can turn the pages. You can pass your eyes over the words. Some things you're going to get. Some things you're not."

"And me? Am I—?"

"A book?"

He nods, brown eyes shiny with hope.

"More like a pamphlet."

"That's funny. Ha, ha."

"Tri-fold."

Timothy smiles that gorgeous smile. He pulls her close, thinks this is his cute cue for a kiss.

"My mother is dying."

"Oh my God!" he cries. "Oh, I'm so sorry."

"I'll live, but I've got to go home."

Last night, Aunt Pen called out of the blue to say, "The cancer has gone to the brain."

Sam ran a pen across a notepad, trying to think of a response that wouldn't sound like relief.

"I met with the doctor. He gives her three months."

"Wait, you're in Ware?"

"I've moved back," Aunt Pen said, judgment creeping into her voice. "I'll be here for as long as it takes."

Timothy takes her hand. A customer by the party dresses glances their way. "I'll come with you."

"Are you out of—?"

"I want to. I want to be with you."

Sam wheels into a checkout line, smiling, like after a mouthful of something way too sweet. She wants to say no, but Timothy, she has to admit, may be useful: a reminder, a buffer, or even a useful source to which (in a pinch) she might refer.

Here Is Ware

HERE IS WARE, the sign on the side of the road proclaims. "Home of the Ware High Wolves, Lacrosse State Champions, 1999."

Out of the corner of her eye, Sam spies Timothy nervously smoothing down his beach-colored hair. Blithe hair, she thinks with an irrational twinge of resentment.

"Seriously?" Timothy says. "The Ware Wolves?"

"If you grew up here, you'd see that crazy doesn't need a moon."

Timothy laughs as he turns onto Market Street, which is lined as usual with white lights and wreaths. There is the Douglass fir, the quaint clock tower, Santa in his glass house gazebo. A horse clops toward them, towing a family cozy in a carriage. They pass the old specialty shop—The Golden Egg—where Sam used to work. She looks at the entrance, thinks she spies Mrs. Sansevere wrapping something delicate at the counter.

"This is neat," Timothy says, voice free of irony. "You know—quaint."

Quaint. Sam's heart stirs—or does it bristle? This is a town that's always looked good for the holiday act. How hard can it be to see right through it?

Badge of Honor

It's seven degrees outside, but Mother's trailer is the tropics. Leah stands in cut off shorts and a bikini top at the sink, the water running. "Make yourselves at home," she says, nodding at a pot of coffee. In the living room, the TV storms.

"Where is she?" Sam asks, smoke burning her throat.

"In the back room." Leah turns, approaches with soap foamy hands. "Why hello young man!" She smiles, hard lines jabbing down her face.

"Hi," Timothy says, averting his eyes. "You must be—"

"Insane? What was your first clue?"

Timothy glances at Sam, and Leah bursts into laughter. "It's just a joke. A little ha-ha to get us through the day."

Sam steps toward the bedroom, moving before she loses her nerve.

It's been kind of a bad morning," Leah says, lowering her voice.

"Samantha, do you want me—?" Timothy is standing by the door, wringing his hands, and she is delighted—perversely so—to see him so deep over his head.

"Stay here." Sam points to the remote, the brown marshmallow sofa. "Please."

When she opens the bedroom door, Sam finds the bed made and Mother naked in a rocking chair, arms folded, veiny legs crossed, flaccid slabs of flesh one atop the other. She can't keep from putting hand over mouth. More than anything, she wants to turn and plunge back into the frigid afternoon, swim through wind and flurries, north, north, to a place by the pole where life doesn't pulse. But she does not—cannot—move, held by some invisible hand, two fingers redirecting her chin, thumb forcing down her lower lip so that a "How are you feeling?" can trickle into the room.

"It's the Lord's will," Mother says. "A blessing. He doesn't give everyone time to set their house in order."

Sam glances at a cloud-walking Jesus on the wall and does her best not to smile. "Would you like to meet Timothy?"

"Who?"

"My boyfriend. I told you. I sent pictures."

Mother rocks in the chair. Is Sam supposed to read the action as acquiescence? An acknowledgment of a life of piss-poor mothering? "I'm not ready," she says after a long, silent time.

"I can come back."

"I'm not ready." Mother rubs a palm against her nose. When she coughs, Sam can't bear to look. "There's some money on the dresser. Why don't you go have a ball?"

At Oberlin, bad parents are a badge of honor. For study breaks, Lily and Miranda often make a pot of tea and sit crosslegged on their beds, firing darkly comic stories like cannonballs back and forth. Reading at her desk, Sam looks up on occasion with a smile, avoiding the temptation to jump into the good-natured battle.

"Go on, take it. The holidays . . ."

Now, Sam has half a mind to snap some pictures, scoop up the bills and bus it back to Ohio, so she can blow her roommates clean out of the water—put all of their horror stories to shame.

Chocolate in the Hand

They're at Neon, an upscale restaurant at the fancy end of Market—Timothy's treat again. With her boyfriend's blessing, Sam orders a martini, the first sips of which begin to fill her with clarity and calm. She wants to be good to Timothy—approach his lofty level for once. She smiles, touches his hand across the table. They talk about the trauma of final exams, the winter term offerings, a newspaper internship Timothy will start in the spring. She asks what Christmas is going to be like with his family. "I figure I should be prepared."

Timothy's family, he reminds her, are total Anglophiles. Each year, they gather for a traditional Christmas—a golden goose, buttery Brussels sprouts, figgy pudding and all the rest. "My father can be annoying," he says. "Be warned: at some point, he's going to trap you in the rec room and talk you to death about all his model battleships."

"My father . . ." Sam says, common sense telling her to stop while the gin, which (curiously) is nearly gone, urges her to give Timothy's circumscribed world a good crack on the skull.

"Is something wrong?"

"My father is not a people person. He's more of a . . . peephole person."

Timothy furrows his brow. He opens his mouth twice before asking in a low, pained voice: "What are you saying?"

"I'm trying to tell you."

"Samantha . . ."

"If you don't like it—"

"What? Are you breaking up—?"

"Why would you say—?"

"Sometimes—and this might not be fair—I get the impression that you just . . . well, you just put up with me."

Sam looks at the drop of gin still lodged in the thin throat of her glass. "People like you," she says. "People like you have it all: gobs of money, siblings and cousins who are best friends for life, parents who'd give an arm and leg to make your dreams come true. Someone asks you the story of your life and you can say, I went from here to here and now—voila!—I'm here. All I've got is bits and pieces. Shards. They prick and jab if you even think about arranging them."

"I'm sorry," Timothy says, eyes soft like chocolate in the hand.

"What are you looking at?"

"What?"

"You're just, I don't know—staring."

"I didn't mean—I'm just, you know, you're lovely and hurt and I'm looking—"

"Well stop. It creeps me out."

Timothy smiles, but she knows it's a sloppy bandage over a terrible wound. A part of her feels sorry for this soft, sincere boy who up until now has lived a trouble-free life. A part of her rests easy, knowing her tough talk is a favor.

"I'm truly sorry," he says, turning to his menu. "Did you decide what you're going to have?"

Sam sits there, the book of entrées heavy like the history of the world in her hands.

What Can I Say?

"Hello?" Sam says, pushing back the open door of the trailer. She smells smoke, coffee—spies the pot on the kitchen counter.

"Who's there?" A familiar voice—not Aunt Leah's. Confident. Defiant. With a firm pinch of accusation. "Who is it?"

"Aunt Pen, it's me. Samantha."

Sam closes the door to infernal cold and, zipping down her coat, begins to adjust to infernal heat. In the kitchen, Aunt Pen is putting away groceries, the refrigerator door a thick sheet of ice between them.

"How's Mom?"

Aunt Pen looks at her with hard, dark eyes. "It's been a difficult morning."

"Is she—?"

"Resting. My sister is resting."

Aunt Pen sinks down behind the sheet of ice, and Sam fiddles with the zipper on her coat. She'd almost brought Timothy with her this morning, instead of sending him with *The Times* to the Cup O' Soul. Would his presence have saved her from this icy blast? Would he have only made things worse?

"I brought out some things, a few small boxes," her aunt says, standing again and nodding toward the living room. "It's not too soon to start . . ." Her eyes momentarily soften. "Anyway, see what you want."

Sam takes a cup of coffee into the living room and sinks into the brown marshmallow couch. In the first box is a pad of golden rod, half filled with stick people under incredible egg yolk suns; an *I Can Read Book* with the final pages torn out; a headless Barbie doll with filed down breasts; a series of dark, tapered stones—arrowheads from her two-week stint as a child archeologist. In the other container is a throw pillow under which rests a pristine ballerina music box, a gift (she remembers) from Aunt Pen. There's a report card too—Ware High, senior year, As across the board, a comment from Ms. Flores: "Samantha is poised to soar!"

Aunt Pen comes into the room, sits across from her in a folding chair, mug of coffee like a pet in her lap. "Find anything you like?"

"This is it? This is all I have?"

"Your Mom's never been much of a collector."

"She's never been much of a mother."

Aunt Pen puts her coffee on a tray table and reaches into a nearby laundry basket. Sam pages through *The Fire Cat*. According to the kindly woman who befriends him, Pickles is not a good cat. He is not a bad cat. He is a good cat and a bad cat.

"Maybe you should take a leave," Aunt Pen says.

Sam looks up to see her aunt holding a pale sling of silk—Mother's underwear.

"Stay home this spring." Aunt Pen glances towards the bedroom before softly adding, "It won't be long."

"It's senior year."

"I've taken a leave from my job."

At school, Sam is busy trying to make a life for herself. She has a senior thesis to write—an examination of the abolitionist movement in Ohio through the lens of the famous case of John Price, the runaway slave captured in Oberlin before being taken back by a group of angry blacks and whites. She has graduate school to attend—"We'll get you into Virginia," Professor Fuller has told her more than once. She has a boyfriend, a good, clean-cut boy who, for reasons she can't fathom, loves almost everything about her.

"You have…what can I say—"

"Yes, I get it. A responsibility."

"That's a good word."

When Sam was a little girl, Aunt Pen's house was the haven on the hill, a place of warmth and treats and smiles. Lights off, cozy in the bottom bunk, she'd listen to her cousin Grace frame one of their fun days together, a monologue punctuated by a giddy series of "Wasn't that greats?" At such times, it was not difficult for Sam to imagine herself as a sister, a daughter—a bone fide member of the family. Now, it's clear Aunt Pen has turned against her, is changing the past—recasting roles—before Sam's eyes. Mother is now the martyr, her aunt the dutiful sister. And Sam? She's the ungrateful daughter, the spoiled girl at the fancy school who thinks she can learn her way to freedom from a family she's always despised.

"How's Grace?" she asks, eyes hiding in her meager box of stuff.

"She could be better." Aunt Pen says. "We all could be better."

Breakdown

WEGMANS—BRIGHT AND VAST, is packed with holiday shoppers at 10:30 pm, but since Sam and Timothy are only here for some cola and trail mix for tomorrow's trip to Connecticut, they zip through the express line and back into below zero air, a head-down sprint to Timothy's Toyota, which doesn't want to start. Sam steps into a stiff fist of wind, meets her boyfriend at the front of the car, where he scratches furiously at his ski cap before sliding tentative fingers under the hood.

"I think you have to pop it from the inside," Sam says. It's cold—so damn cold; in another context, Timothy's incompetence might be endearing.

She's right (he thanks her profusely), and Timothy is back, knees against the bumper, fingers under the hood, feeling and feeling before finding—and comprehending—the latch.

"Ha, I know this much," he says, blowing into bare hands.

Together, they stare at the steel and plastic organs, the soft twisty arcs of hoses and wires—the whole dreadful geometry of the thing.

"Dead battery?" Timothy suggests, the question swirling stupidly around them like another gust of wind. Sam takes a deep breath, feels her nose hairs freeze. She goes back into the store to call AAA. Twenty minutes later, the tow truck arrives and Mac—her cousin—climbs from the cab.

"Hey, hey, didn't know you was back this way," he says. Despite the cold, he wears just a ball cap and a sweatshirt. His ears are mauve. A trickle of clear snot fingers down toward chapped lips. Sam meets his eyes, tries to find lingering guilt for the recklessness that took the bright blue eye of her cousin Grace.

"Just passing through," Sam says. Wincing, she turns to introduce Timothy.

"A real pleasure." Mac grabs her boyfriend's hand—aggressive, but not unfriendly.

Timothy blushes, nods, stands in a daze while Mac takes crocodile clamps, pinches the terminals on the battery. Positive, negative. He talks about his younger brother Mark, who celebrated his release from jail for a third DUI by buying a cat from the shelter and promptly dying it blue.

"Um, why?" Sam asks, shivering like mad.

"Because, I think, it was tan."

"That's crazy," Sam says.

"No, Sammy. It's royally fucked up!"

Sam laughs—she can't help herself. Timothy has moved a few feet away, hands jammed in pockets, feet trying to dance away the cold.

Mac says, "Okay, why don't you go give her a try."

Timothy climbs in and turns the key. The car roars to life. "Saved!" he cries, returning to Mac, who is easing down the hood.

Back inside the car, hands on the heating vent, Sam watches Timothy sign the form. As Mac rips the receipt, her boyfriend goes into his wallet for a couple of bills. Her cousin shakes his head, claps Timothy on the shoulder. Despite the blast of heat, despite the thickness of the windshield, Sam can hear Mac say "Merry Christmas!" before climbing into the cab and driving away.

"What a nice guy," Timothy says, settling behind the wheel.

Sam stares into the roaring vent. Heat may be invisible, but all she sees is red.

Dodging a Bullet

Timothy has sprung for the motel—nothing fancy, but haven enough from the horror show around them. For the first two nights, he's been the perfect Christian gentleman, changing into pajamas behind the bathroom door, kissing her once tenderly on the mouth, before sliding into his own twin. Tonight, though, when Sam clicks off the desk lamp, there's the rustling of covers, and he's right beside her.

"I just really need to hug you," he whispers, breath minty and clean.

He strokes her naked shoulder, fondles a spaghetti strap while Sam speaks, the groups of words—"I can't wait to leave," "My aunt is a traitor," "My mother is a pathetic lump of dung," "My father . . ."—between them like so many bubbles in a stupid Sunday cartoon.

"I know, I know," Timothy says, lightly drawing with a finger between her shoulder blades.

"You don't know," she says shifting away from him. "My father, when I was little, he, he . . . saw me by the win—"

"You said."

"No, there's more." She owes him the truth he does not want. For his patience, his rectitude. The truth without the act. "And there were other times, things . . ." But is this a favor? A curse? A simple mode of defense?

"How do you know? What other things?"

"You don't believe me?"

"I believe in you."

In the dark, she could be anywhere. The advancing hands could be Timothy's, or worse.

"I can't see you," she cries.

The weight of an old dream moves upon her.

"It doesn't matter. Nothing matters for now."

She finds it hard to breathe, harder still as hands begin to dive. "I don't think—"

She's shushed with one kiss then another, soft at first and then a ruthless corkscrew. Before things go further, she reaches down, forms a fist around the plank in the pajamas. Pull, pull. A memory of Father in Horseheads at a trap shooting range, his barrel up and roaring. Pull, pull. Sam on a cold stone bench, knees to her chin, hands mashed against her ears.

"Ah, Ah!" she hears—an old voice, a young. "Shit, stop, wait—no, go!"

Pull, pull. Father, a dead eye, pierced one pigeon, then the one right after. Both of them watched a spray of dark red rain over a far-reaching field of brown.

Life. Sorry.

Aunt Doreen sits across from them, eyes shiny as hard candy. Sam pushes her back fiercely against the bars of the chair. For several moments, her aunt simply smiles and blinks.

Then, at last, a shout: "I'm just so happy you've come!"

As if they'd had a choice, Sam ambushed with a phone call that morning when she was still coming to in the motel bed. "Is this you?" the voice cried. "You're in town, and you aren't going to visit? What's wrong with you?" Aunt Pen, it turned out, gave Aunt Doreen the number—a sneaky act of vengeance, if ever there was one.

Aunt Doreen turns now to Timothy, whose head is down like a school boy afraid of being called upon. "Are you really from Connecticut? Would you like something to drink? What would you like? I could make coffee. I've made sugar cookies! Have you eaten lunch? How about spiral ham? It's a pig going round in circles, ha ha!"

"I'm … good," Timothy says, smiling nervously. "Thank you, ma'am."

"I see." Aunt Doreen picks at her plaid skirt like it's a slide guitar. "Sam probably told you I'm a little off my rocker. Don't take food from the crazy lady . . ."

"We just ate," Sam says. The truth is, she could eat a pig, curly tail and all.

"I'm not going to poison you. I take my medicine."

"Aunt Doreen—"

"No, no," she says, slicing the air with her fingernails. "Don't ever worry about me. I have contained right here in this old noggin the secret to life. How old am I? Forty? If I can keep it together for thirty some more years, I'll be all set. Isn't that what the Lord says? Keep it together. Really, it's kind of a game." She slaps her lap. "Like Life . . . or the other one—Sorry. I'm more than half way to my heavenly home."

They agree on tap water for refreshment. Sam, trying not to be obvious, meanders to the doorway of the kitchen to watch her aunt fill the snowman tumblers. They'll stay fifteen more minutes, Sam vows. Fifteen more minutes of freakishness and then they can be free, full speed ahead, the Toyota firing out of town like a rocket to the sun.

"How's your mother?"

"Not well."

"I never see her. Don't go out much. They have a van that picks me up for church."

Sam nods. She can't think of a single thing to do with her mouth but scream.

"Penny says it's cancer. That's such a terrible thing. But it's God's plan." Aunt Doreen takes a long drink of water. "Just like when the lovebirds met. You know, your father and mother. He was so handsome and he had that car, which one do you call it? A real fancy one . . ."

"Corvette?" Timothy says.

Aunt Doreen beams. "Yes! Maybe. It's got one of those front ends . . . like a playground slide?"

"Right. That's the one."

Out of the corner of her eye, Sam sees Timothy move forward to the edge of his chair, hands together as if in prayer.

"God's plan that he rented the house next door. God's plan that your mother just lost that other boy and was wearing that pretty dress he said looked real nice. God's plan that he had money, a good job, and he liked to take her places she'd never been before. God's plan they married and had you, the twinkle in their eyes. God's plan the hard times came. God's plan that he had some other place to go. God's plan that she got sick and you came home and

I called you up and you're here right now, the first time in I don't know how many years."

Sam crosses her arms. She presses both feet on the floor.

"I was the flower girl at the wedding, and your mother, she had that beautiful long blue dress and her hair just so, but she reached hugged me, said she was so happy and I thought—and I still think—how could that face with those words never not be true? You know what I'm saying? Am I saying what I mean?"

Later, as they rise to leave, Aunt Doreen disappears in the kitchen, returning moments later with a tin foiled plate. "Take some cookies home. You can examine them at your leisure. Enjoy them or throw them in the trash. I'll never know. Merry Christmas!"

In the car, Sam slouches with great relief. She peels back the foil. "I'm so starved."

The heater blows full blast, and her coat is up to her neck, yet she still feels the cold, the death of all the world. Timothy, to his credit, has kept his composure, although he looks now close to the color of freshly fallen snow.

He pulls out onto the main road—Victory Highway, Sam thinks with a smile. After a few precious moments of peace, Sam returns to the cookies and works a hand under the foil, drawing out what might be a Santa Claus. Tarot cards, a memory of her and Zoey at a fortune teller's on a shopping trip to Ithaca. "You will go places," the woman said, her voice disappointingly matter-of-fact. The Five of Cups is the card Sam remembers, the slumped, black-cloaked figure before spilled wine, receptacles like hourglasses on their sides. Sam remembers the woman saying something about loss, which made all kinds of sense to her at the time.

"They look good," she says now.

Timothy pulls to the shoulder before the highway ramp. He leans over, takes the Santa from her hand, turns it in his hand for signs of aberration.

"It's red and white," Sam says. "That's normal."

"But there's no face."

"That's not unusual, is it? Wouldn't it be worse if it had one of those loopy doopy smiles?"

Timothy sniffs the cookie, taps it against his lips. Sam studies him intently—the trembling fingers, the eyes wet with both worry and desire. Without further drama, he plunges the cookie into his mouth. "There!" he says, chewing obscenely. "What's done is done."

Langston, Charles Langston, a free black and one of the men who rescued that slave John Price, said at his trial, "We have a common humanity," and that is the sentiment that flies into Sam's head as she puts a hand on Timothy's leg, pulls him close, kisses him hard. His hands move to her shoulders, through her flames of hair. She closes her eyes and, in the dark again, tongues the warm hole before her, flicking for sweet icing, for any and all of those softening crumbs.

Credits

"Mei Wenti" was previously published in *REAL* (Summer/Fall 2008).

"Search" was previously published in *Fiction Fix* (June 2012).

"A Night at The Orr House" was previously published in *Stickman Review* (Fall 2016).

"If No One Was Strange" was previously published in *Main Street Rag* (Summer 2017).

"Here Is Ware" was previously published in *Novella-T* (June 2014).

Fomite

About Fomite

A fomite is a medium capable of transmitting infectious organisms from one individual to another.

"The activity of art is based on the capacity of people to be infected by the feelings of others." Tolstoy, *What Is Art?*

Writing a review on Amazon, Good Reads, Shelfari, Library Thing or other social media sites for readers will help the progress of independent publishing. To submit a review, go to the book page on any of the sites and follow the links for reviews. Books from independent presses rely on reader-to-reader communications. For more information or to order any of our books, visit http://www.fomitepress.com/FOMITE/Our_Books.html

More Titles from Fomite...

Novels
Joshua Amses — *Ghatsr*
Joshua Amses — *During This, Our Nadir*
Joshua Amses — *Raven or Crow*
Joshua Amses — *The Moment Before an Injury*
Jaysinh Birjepatel — *The Good Muslim of Jackson Heights*
Jaysinh Birjepatel — *Nothing Beside Remains*
David Brizer — *Victor Rand*
Paula Closson Buck — *Summer on the Cold War Planet*
Dan Chodorkoff — *Loisaida*
David Adams Cleveland — *Time's Betrayal*
Jaimee Wriston Colbert — *Vanishing Acts*
Roger Coleman — *Skywreck Afternoons*
Marc Estrin — *Hyde*
Marc Estrin — *Kafka's Roach*
Marc Estrin — *Speckled Vanities*
Zdravka Evtimova — *In the Town of Joy and Peace*

Fomite

Fomite

Bob Sommer — *A Great Fullness*
Tom Walker — *A Day in the Life*
Susan V. Weiss —*My God, What Have We Done?*
Peter M. Wheelwright — *As It Is On Earth*
Suzie Wizowaty — *The Return of Jason Green*

Poetry

Anna Blackmer — *Hexagrams*
Antonello Borra — *Alfabestiario*
Antonello Borra — *AlphaBetaBestiaro*
Sue D. Burton — *Little Steel*
David Cavanagh— *Cycling in Plato's Cave*
James Connolly — *Picking Up the Bodies*
Greg Delanty — *Loosestrife*
Mason Drukman — *Drawing on Life*
J. C. Ellefson — *Foreign Tales of Exemplum and Woe*
Tina Escaja/Mark Eisner — *Caida Libre/Free Fall*
Anna Faktorovich — *Improvisational Arguments*
Barry Goldensohn — *Snake in the Spine, Wolf in the Heart*
Barry Goldensohn — *The Hundred Yard Dash Man*
Barry Goldensohn — *The Listener Aspires to the Condition of Music*
R. L. Green — *When You Remember Deir Yassin*
Gail Holst-Warhaft — *Lucky Country*
Raymond Luczak — *A Babble of Objects*
Kate Magill — *Roadworthy Creature, Roadworthy Craft*
Tony Magistrale — *Entanglements*
Andreas Nolte — *Mascha: The Poems of Mascha Kaléko*
Sherry Olson — *Four-Way Stop*
David Polk — *Drinking the River*
Aristea Papalexandrou/Philip Ramp — *Μας προσπερνά/It's Passing Us By*
Janice Miller Potter — *Meanwell*
Philip Ramp — *The Melancholy of a Life as the Joy of Living It
        Slowly Chills*
Joseph D. Reich — *Connecting the Dots to Shangrila*
Joseph D. Reich — *The Hole That Runs Through Utopia*

Fomite

Joseph D. Reich — *The Housing Market*
Joseph D. Reich — *The Derivation of Cowboys and Indians*
Kennet Rosen and Richard Wilson — *Gomorrah*
Fred Rosenblum — *Vietnumb*
David Schein — *My Murder and Other Local News*
Harold Schweizer — *Miriam's Book*
Scott T. Starbuck — *Industrial Oz*
Scott T. Starbuck — *Hawk on Wire*
Scott T. Starbuck — *Carbonfish Blues*
Seth Steinzor — *Among the Lost*
Seth Steinzor — *To Join the Lost*
Susan Thomas — *The Empty Notebook Interrogates Itself*
Susan Thomas — *In the Sadness Museum*
Paolo Valesio/Todd Portnowitz — *La Mezzanotte di Spoleto/ Midnight in Spoleto*
Sharon Webster — *Everyone Lives Here*
Tony Whedon — *The Tres Riches Heures*
Tony Whedon — *The Falkland Quartet*
Claire Zoghb — *Dispatches from Everest*

Stories
Jay Boyer — *Flight*
Michael Cocchiarale — *Still Time*
Michael Cocchiarale — *Here Is Ware*
Neil Connelly — *In the Wake of Our Vows*
Catherine Zobal Dent — *Unfinished Stories of Girls*
Zdravka Evtimova —*Carts and Other Stories*
John Michael Flynn — *Off to the Next Wherever*
Derek Furr — *Semitones*
Derek Furr — *Suite for Three Voices*
Elizabeth Genovise — *Where There Are Two or More*
Andrei Guriuanu — *Body of Work*
Zeke Jarvis — *In A Family Way*
Arya Jenkins — *Blue Songs in an Open Key*
Jan Englis Leary — *Skating on the Vertical*

Fomite

Marjorie Maddox — *What She Was Saying*
William Marquess — *Boom-shacka-lacka*
Gary Miller — *Museum of the Americas*
Jennifer Anne Moses — *Visiting Hours*
Martin Ott — *Interrogations*
Jack Pulaski — *Love's Labours*
Charles Rafferty — *Saturday Night at Magellan's*
Ron Savage — *What We Do For Love*
Fred Skolnik— *Americans and Other Stories*
Lynn Sloan — *This Far Is Not Far Enough*
L.E. Smith — *Views Cost Extra*
Caitlin Hamilton Summie — *To Lay To Rest Our Ghosts*
Susan Thomas — *Among Angelic Orders*
Tom Walker — *Signed Confessions*
Silas Dent Zobal — *The Inconvenience of the Wings*

Odd Birds

Micheal Breiner — *the way none of this happened*
J. C. Ellefson — *Under the Influence*
David Ross Gunn — *Cautionary Chronicles*
Andrei Guriuanu and Teknari — *The Darkest City*
Gail Holst-Warhaft — *The Fall of Athens*
Roger Leboitz — *A Guide to the Western Slopes and the Outlying Area*
dug Nap— *Artsy Fartsy*
Delia Bell Robinson — *A Shirtwaist Story*
Peter Schumann — *Bread & Sentences*
Peter Schumann — *Charlotte Salomon*
Peter Schumann — *Faust 3*
Peter Schumann — *Planet Kasper, Volumes One and Two*
Peter Schumann — *We*

Plays

Stephen Goldberg — *Screwed and Other Plays*
Michele Markarian — *Unborn Children of America*

 Fomite

www.ingramcontent.com/pod-product-compliance
Lightning Source LLC
Chambersburg PA
CBHW050355190726
48284CB00007BB/2300